## *The Fire Was Gone*

She came upon the body of a fieldmouse evidently suffocated by the smoke. She took up a sharp rock, dug a hole in the resisting earth and buried it, weeping silently.

The flames had burned out a near-perfect circle, though with the breeze that had been blowing they should have spread farther, more raggedly into the field. Dale sniffed the air, found no lingering remains of gasoline or oil; she rubbed her hand over blackened grass and smelled her fingers—nothing but the stench of fire gone cold. How then, had the fire been directed, been contained about her and Vic?

She kicked at the rubble and dislodged a stone. Glancing down, she saw in the glow of the flashlight that what she had uncovered wasn't a stone.

"Oh, Willy," she said. "Oh, my poor Willy."

The SOUND OF MIDNIGHT

Tor Books by Charles L. Grant

# CHARLES L. GRANT

# The SOUND OF MIDNIGHT

**TOR HORROR**

A TOM DOHERTY ASSOCIATES BOOK

THE SOUND OF MIDNIGHT

Copyright © 1978 by Charles L. Grant

Reprinted by arrangement with the author

First Tor printing: August 1987

A TOR Book

Published by Tom Doherty Associates, Inc.
49 West 24 Street
New York, N.Y. 10010

ISBN: 0-812-51864-0
CAN. ED.: 0-812-51865-9

Printed in the United States of America

0  9  8  7  6  5  4  3  2  1

## Author's Dedication

For Ed:
  Who found me first and keeps me working,
  And refuses to let me be anything but better;
  Welcome to Oxrun, there's a hearth here for you,
  And a full moon and nightmares,
    and a shadow or two.

# CHAPTER
# I

The sun, the afternoon, the park was warm. The last spring chill had died with dawn, and Oxrun Station stored its sweaters into cupboards, mittens into drawers, and watched the traffic on Mainland Road grow thick with campers braving into the mountains. Had it been a weekday, half the schoolchildren would have devised excuses to stay home, and the rest would have spent their learning hours staring out the windows wishing they were somewhere else. It was, however, early June and a green Saturday, with the field in the center of the park spotted with shrill games of baseball, stubborn remnants of football, stampedes of tag over grass that refused to be beaten. The winding tarmac walks became lanes for carriages, trails for bicycles, paths for couples to leave as they found and rediscovered places behind the shrubs and beneath the hickory where they could

1

spread their blankets and promise the moon. Redwood-and-concrete benches floated in and out of twisting shade, while a refreshment kiosk offered the season's first chocolate cone. An old man with a gray canvas sack poked listlessly with a pointed stick at last year's leaves; another leaned against a sapling and clucked to the squirrels.

Only the water in the pond was cold.

Despite the new broad canopy that blended all the trees into one, Dale could glimpse spears of sunlight captured in the water as she crossed the lower field, avoiding the children, ignoring the shrieks that frightened the birds. When she had been the age of the players in the park, she sat on a swing behind High Street Grade School and told her troubles to the dusty red brick. Sometimes it actually worked, but more often it only confused her, and it wasn't until she had grown and left and returned again that she realized it had been the solitude she was after, not the comfort of faded false stone.

Now, in the sun and the warm, there was the pond.

It was a bloated L, large enough to permit a small rowboat or two, small enough to grant the average swimmer the prize of crossing its width. Because of the spring that fed it, however, only a few dared more than wade, and so it was generally shunned until December froze it and brought out the skates.

Leaving the field and the games behind, then, she followed a worn, narrow path until she reached the band of mown grass and weeds that bordered the black water. Standing quietly for a moment on the high bank, she watched a green-capped drake feeding in the shallows while his drab mate and anxious young clustered a few yards distant. Then she turned right and followed the edge until she was facing east and the village was at her back. A lonely elm had punched into the center of a half-circle clearing, and she sat on one exposed root, her view of the water unobstructed except for a treed finger of land halfway between her and the far shore. When the drake finally stopped its bobbing and settled himself with a preening shake, she smiled and saluted him silently.

A light breath of wind ruffled her thin blue blouse, shifted the broad cuffs of her slacks to cover her shoes. She shivered, though she didn't feel the cold, and opened a paper bag out of which she lifted her sandwich lunch. She was trying not to think, rather to concentrate on the taste of the ham and the lettuce and the freshly baked rye Mrs. Inness had brought to the shop that morning. And when that failed, she poked out a tiny mirror from her purse and tried to put sense back into the more-blond-than-brown hair she'd hoped keeping short would make easier to manage. But the mirror stayed on her faintly green eyes, and they were frowning, half in anger, half in worry.

A quick gust from the north intensified the cries of the games, dusting her gratefully until it and they returned to the background. She grabbed a stone and threw it viciously into the water, the sound of its sinking decidedly unsatisfactory.

It had promised to be a good day right from the beginning. She'd slept well, showered and dressed to the accompaniment of her slightly flat alto, had even taken time to eat a rare full breakfast; she walked instead of ran the few long blocks to the store, and was whistled at by an unseen passenger in a speeding car.

Good omens all, and capped by the brilliance of the sun that rose over the park.

After opening the shop, she was given a few blessed minutes to herself before Bella Inness arrived. It wasn't, she'd thought guiltily, that the old woman was actually hurting sales, far from it, but she was too steeped in the store's short traditions to give her full approval to the changes Dale had made. Bartlett's Toys had been her parents' business, a neighbor's family's before that, and had always carried nothing but children's toys, toddlers' clothes, and a select line of demure greeting cards. Dale had realized the nature of competition as soon as she'd taken over, however, and eliminated the clothes and cards and replaced them with games and recreational oddities that would appeal to more than just kids. The fact that the change was successful irritated Mrs. Inness, and a day seldom failed to end without some mention of memories' sacrilege.

It was a friendly though uneasy relationship, based in part on the fact that she had promised her father that no matter what happened to anyone in the family, someone must be sure to keep Bella on the job: she had no one of her own, and without the store she would probably fall into rapid decline. In more ways than one, the store was her life. Friendly, and uneasy; and when Bella had pushed her inevitable broadstriped dress through the door that morning, Dale had tensed, waiting for the opening salvo, the crack, the sniping from the protection of old age and gray hair.

But there'd been nothing but a laughing greeting, a cheek offered for a passing sterile kiss. And the morning had drifted lazily without a hint of trouble.

She reached down and yanked at a tuft of grass. An ant scrambled along a blade and she shook it gently to the ground where it hesitated before moving off purposefully in the direction she'd interrupted.

A good day.

Until Ed McPherson, psychiatrist and chess-set collector, changed it. He came into the store as she was working on the display case beneath the counter by the entrance, where she also kept the register. He'd entered as he always had—slowly, deliberately, his bespectacled puffed face turned intently toward the case and the chessmen arranged within. He'd nodded as she moved aside, examined the pieces while pulling on the fall of brown hair that swept down and over his brow.

"Nothing new," she'd said brightly, and he'd frowned.

"You're sure about that?"

"Well, if I don't know, who does?" she'd said, forcing a laugh, hoping that for once he'd loosen his professional straitjacket, a metaphorical garment donned, she thought, since the death of his wife at home, found drowned in the bathtub, a tragic accident. Yet she always anticipated his coming because of his intense pleasure in the exotic chessmen she brought in from as many cultures as possible, and at the same time dreaded their conversations because he made her feel as though she was in his office, on the couch or wherever he placed his patients, spilling out her life story while he grunted and took notes.

"Nothing from Dave Campbell?"

His wife, Elinor, he'd once told her, never played chess and thought his collection ridiculous.

Now she was dead, and Ed was . . .

"Nothing from Dave Campbell?" he repeated.

"Nope," she said. "He hasn't brought any of his things in to me for a while, in fact. Certainly not a new chess set." And she was startled when the psychiatrist scowled and left without speaking.

"Well, good-by to you, too," she'd muttered as she watched him cross the street without regard for traffic. "Killjoy."

Her mood lightened, however, when Willy Campbell, Dave's son, came in just before twelve and headed directly for the ship models in the back left corner. Bella, standing by the counter, adjusted her bifocals and plumped her sagging bosom. "Watch his coat carefully, Dale," she whispered, loudly enough for the boy to hear. "He gets fat when he leaves those boxes."

"Bella, leave the boy alone."

"He's too young for them things," had been the answer. "He's only nine or ten, you know. He can't do all that little stuff with the rigging and things."

"Bella, for crying out loud, his father probably helps him."

Bella glared at the reprimand, shoved her away and down the aisle where she hovered at the boy's shoulder until he glanced up, smiled and waved to Dale. Then he picked up a box nearly as large as himself and, shaking off Mrs. Inness' "May I assist you, young man?'' he struggled to the counter and set it down.

"Willy," Dale said, "this one is going to take a hundred years, you know that? It's a clipper ship, right?"

"I know, Miss Bartlett," he said. "I can tell by the picture."

She shook open the largest paper sack and eased the box in. "Your dad going to help you with this?"

Willy sobered. "He never does, Miss Bartlett. I do it all myself. I learn better that way."

Bella, who'd stationed herself by the door, snorted.

"Well, I do!" the boy protested. "I do it all myself. All."

"I'm sure you do, Willy," Dale said, handing over the awkward package. "Mrs. Inness, would you open the door for this young man?"

Willy grinned and waited until Bella complied. Then, with one foot out, he stopped and looked up at her. "May I assist you, young man?" he said, laughed, and ran to the sidewalk.

If the door had not been on a spring, Bella would have slammed it. Instead, she fisted her hands on her hips and glared at Dale. "Spoiled little monster. You shouldn't be so friendly with them, Dale. They'll turn on you like snakes."

Dale blinked, not sure of the allusion.

"Your father, now, would never have—"

"My father is dead, Bella."

"Dale! So soon in the grave and already you're forgetting—"

"Three years isn't soon, and I'm forgetting nothing. Now why don't you bring out more of those bookshelf games. We've too many of the same ones on display. Change it around a little.''

Mrs. Inness' hand lifted, and Dale was sure it'd been heading for the doorknob. Instead, it attempted to pat some dignity into her bulk as she turned and headed stiffly back toward the storeroom.

Poor Will, she thought as she tossed another stone in the water. Poor me.

For a moment, then, she wished that Vic were with her. Vic, who taught the kids in the high school that teachers weren't all ogres, and who tried to teach her that it wasn't a crime to enjoy life and living. He had never proposed, not in so many words, but she knew that the words were there, waiting, until she had gotten over being afraid that he might leave her, too.

It was not unusual, she thought when her wish for Vic faded, that there had been nothing in her life to prepare her for the airplane crash that had taken both her parents' lives on the side of a Colorado mountain— but neither was there a Bartlett tradition of prolonged and agonizing mourning. It had been tragic, and she had cried herself to sleep in the house now hers for weeks on end, then only sporadically; but it was now done. Over. Just like the decision to postpone graduate school to work at the store until a buyer came along.

And when he had, she refused to sell.

She had discovered joy in the business: clothes were things that people needed to buy, but a game, a toy . . . she grinned at herself.

Much of that, she was forced to admit, had been

Vic's doing. Often, he came into the store and opened the boxes of things he hadn't seen before, spread the game/toy/puzzle on the counter and spent hours trying to figure it out, or watching it click into motion, or simply laughing at the mind behind the creation. At first she had thought him childish, until his laughter had become infectious and his delight in the new and the bright and the maddeningly complex had taken her and transformed her.

The buyer had been refused because her mourning had been done.

And Vic was still there, waiting patiently for her to make up her mind. Not a martyr to love, because he dated others without apology; but a friend waiting to be more, whenever she decided it was time and she was ready.

Games. Toys. Another grin, and her anger at Bella, well-meaning Bella with her rare small smile, her anger at invoking her parents' memory faded, and was replaced by a brief wash of sympathy for Willy Campbell, who tried so hard, too hard, to be older than he was. Not that the other children who frequented the shop didn't play the adult game, too, but Willy strove rather than played, struggled rather than larked. Were he a genius, a prodigy, he might have pulled it off—but he was the Oxrun average, and nothing he did was able to alter that image in anyone's eyes but his own.

She leaned back and pressed her head against the elm's bark, staring through the lattice that fragmented the sky. Her lunch sat heavily and she chided herself for not bringing anything to drink. Somehow she was going to have to apologize to Bella for embarrassing her in front of the boy. That had been a serious error and she should have know better, but there were days when the woman's intolerance was simply too much to pass over; and if she hated the kids so damned much, why did she bother to stay on?

Another grin. That one was easy. Bella was afraid that without her, Dale would drive the store into bankruptcy, defame the Bartlett reputation, drive the Station into depression, and leave her without an outlet for her grumpiness.

Suddenly the day seemed to be turning again. McPherson was forgiven his stodginess, Bella her suspicions. She sat up and stretched. The drake had assembled his family and was leading it away from her, straight across the center of the pond toward the spit of land that severed the western tip from view. A dragonfly lifted from the low weeds and darted toward her, swerved when she instinctively ducked, and vanished. She remembered the year the water had been clogged with lily pads and the bees that swarmed over the blossoms' white and yellow had stung quite a few of the children playing on the banks. That winter the pond had been drained, the pads killed at the roots and diligently weeded thereafter. Safer, perhaps, but somehow such a body of water seemed naked now without the scattered blotches of green.

A glance at her watch made her gasp silently, grab for the empty bag, and rise. Her legs were stiff, her knees cracked. She stretched again, shook her head vigorously, and turned to cut back through the trees to the Park Street entrance. A single step, and she heard a scream.

At first she thought it her imagination, a squeal of brakes from a nearby street. She listened, but there was nothing; turned, and it came again. When she whirled, the drake was pushing its mate and ducklings rapidly toward the far side of the pond.

A third time, and Dale broke into a run, staying as close to the lip of the bank as she could, staring into the shadows to locate the source of that terror. Now the scream had multiplied, and she could hear splashing and knew that someone had fallen into the water and couldn't get out. A wintercut branch hidden in tall grass tripped her, but she flailed and kept her balance. Across the pond she could see other adults breaking through the trees from the field, heading around the other side. No more than a half dozen, but by their speed she guessed they could see what she could not.

Then she passed the finger of land barely wide enough for three trees abreast and, emerging from the thick underbrush, saw the children standing quietly on the low, muddy bank. She stopped, hesitant, then dashed forward, scattering them as she searched them for familiar faces.

"Carolyn, what's wrong?" she demanded of one small redhead. The girl only stared up at her and began to cry. When she stepped aside, nudging her friends to do the same, Dale saw the body.

A small boy, his face down in the mud, his legs stretched into the water, floating. Leaves were pasted to his hair and the back of his neck. He was drenched, and fully clothed. Without thinking, Dale knelt and turned him over.

"Oh my God, Willy!"

"He wanted a duck, Miss Bartlett," one fearfully small voice said. "He went in to get me a duck and he fell and started making all them noises."

"A monster got him, Miss Bartlett," a quivering, solemn boy told her. "Came right up and grabbed him."

"Did not," another girl said. "The ducks got him, silly."

"Shut up, all of you!" Dale yelled, and they stepped back. Eight of them. Shivering in the hot sun. Clustered like goslings, only a few without tears. Dale carefully wiped the mud from Willy's face, brushed back his hair and with a prayer she really didn't feel, pinched his nose and bent over to blow into his mouth, push his chest, blow, push, blow, push, looking up once to see a man kneel and lift a small scratched wrist. Blow, push, realization growing despite the fight she waged to keep it back.

Footfalls, and someone ordering the children to be taken away, the children protesting meekly and going, an order for the police unnecessary as a siren shattered the dreamlike fuzziness that had settled over the pond. Blow, push, and a hand on her shoulder.

"It's no good, Dale." Softly. Masculine. "It's no good, Dale. The boy's dead."

Blow, push, tears acid but not falling, the taste of mud and pond water.

The hand firmer, forcing her back onto her heels. She reached up and slapped it away. Willy, eyes closed, mud streaks already caking, seemed to pale perceptibly. A fly lighted on his chin, and Dale spun around and vomited.

She heard nothing but her own gagging, felt nothing but the pains in her chest and stomach until a hand, the same hand, pressed a handkerchief into her palm and she wiped her face, scooped cold water into her eyes and forehead. Slowly, then, she lifted her head and stared unseeing at the opposite shore.

"Willy," she said flatly.

The sound of a heavy shoe in mud, and hands cupped beneath her arms and lifted her, unprotesting, led her several yards to the shade of a willow. She saw faces turn away, sorrowful and pitying, torn between concern for her welfare and the spectacle of the boy dead in the mud. There were whispers, but she made no sense of any of them. The hands had released her, and one was slowly rubbing her lower back while the other carefully dried her face with a soft piece of cloth. She wanted to smile her gratitude, but when she worked to position her lips they only tensed, quivered, and her teeth clamped down hard to keep them from screaming.

"It's okay, Dale, it's okay."

She looked up, blinking. To dark hair curled loosely, a tanned, lean face with squinting black eyes and a thick-lipped mouth, a mustache and close-cropped beard hiding the jaw.

"Bella told me you were out here," he said quietly.

"My God, Vic," she said finally. "Vic, I heard him screaming."

She hugged herself tightly but shook her head when he took a step forward. He nodded, fingered a cigarette from his breast pocket and lighted it, handed it to her and waited until she'd choked on the first intake of acrid smoke before lighting one for himself.

"I saw him just this morning, you know. He came

into the shop for one of his models. A big one again, a ship this time. His father must think he can do anything.'' She laughed quickly. A policeman she recognized as Fred Borg was kneeling by the boy's body. He ran a hand carefully over the boy's head, looked at his palm and wiped it on a handkerchief. Then, with some difficulty, he pried open the fingers of the left hand and took something from it. Dale stared, thinking it a stone before realizing it was a tiny figurine. A gift from his father's workshop, she thought as Fred looked it over and dropped it into his shirt pocket before arranging a sheeting over the face while ambulance attendants set up a stretcher. The crowd had grown, and was strangely silent. The children were gone.

''The poor things,'' she said. ''They had to see it, to see such a terrible thing.''

Borg stood and stared in her direction until Vic pointed at his watch, then over his shoulder. The policeman nodded and returned to his grim business.

''Come on, Dale,'' Vic said, taking her shoulder. ''Let's go. There's nothing more you can do here.''

''But—''

''We'll meet Fred at the station. He can take your statement there. Come on, there's no sense in sticking around here.''

''But the children, Vic . . .'' Her last protest, weak and arguable. She reached down automatically for her purse before remembering she'd left it in the clearing.

''What would you do without that thing?'' Vic said, sensing her loss and guiding her through the trees. "Better you should be a kangaroo, then you wouldn't lose it all the time."

She smiled and touched his arm gratefully. When he covered her hand with his, however, she disengaged gently. This was hardly the time for a show of encouragement; and as soon as she thought it, she became angry because she knew that Vic, no matter how hard he pursued her otherwise, would not take advantage. Though reared during the turmoil of a shift in morality, priorities, the new awareness of the world, Vic Blake had remained somehow steadfastly conservative when it came to his treatment of women and his elders. There was almost a continental flair of the gallant in his actions, and though Dale liked to believe she was part of the emerging new woman image, she nevertheless admitted to herself that she enjoyed his quiet, unpretentious attention to small things like doors and chairs and lighting of cigarettes.

"Here," she said, pointing to the elm where she'd taken her lunch.

He motioned her to stay, then loped around the bank and fetched the purse, hefting it as he returned and grinning. "How many guns, Dale? Or is it a howitzer?"

"Just the usual addition to a woman's vanity," she said.

"Dale Bartlett is not vain," he said loudly as they moved off toward the field. "She is sometimes headstrong, too self-confident, a damned good businesswoman—for a woman—but she is definitely not vain!"

Willy. His legs floating. Fist clenched. Faint tinge of red on the back of his head. She couldn't bring herself to contribute to the banter and, when he saw her distress, Vic shoved his suit jacket out of the way and pushed his hands into his trouser pockets.

"He was a nice kid," he said. "When school was over, he and his gang would come over to hang around the freshmen." A hand scratched at his curls, drifted to a habitual stroking of his beard. "They didn't mind him, you know. They didn't mind those little kids. They were a lot smaller, but they acted older, if you know what I mean. We used to have practically classroom sessions right there in the yard."

The field was deserted. At the park's wrought-iron-gate entrance, a policeman stood in front of a small milling crowd, trying without touching to dissuade them from entering. Several people drifted off as Dale and Vic passed, but the more stubborn ones silently remained. At the curb, Vic waited patiently. Directly opposite them was the beginning of High Street, and on the block to their right the grade school the Oxrun children attended. It was an old brick two-story giant that had been there, it was said, since the Civil War; there was a playground behind it, then a small pocket park, and the Station's new library that fronted Williamston Pike. Bookends, Dale thought, as they crossed the street and began walking west along High. New library, old school, and both had now lost a strayed, enthusiastic friend.

"Hey," Vic said quietly, and took her shoulder, pulled her close while the tears, released at last, coursed and her breath gasped out in silent sobs. They had crossed Centre Street and had walked another block to Fox Road before she had cried out her remorse and mopped her face with the handkerchief she hadn't yet returned. Away from the businesses, now, the streets were quiet, fronted with homes Victorian and colonial in large and antique freshly painted splendor. Between here and Mainland Road were the homes of the village's middle class and those whose traditions of wealth didn't lend themselves to the small estates ranging on the far side of the park. They wandered, then, under the comforting whispering of elm and maple, the occasional willow, the clumps of birch, no talk. Wondered in bitter silence why children had to die.

Finally they were standing at the corner of Northland and Steuben in front of the gray marble bulk of the Station's high school. Vic glanced up at the tall shaded windows and pulled her to the broad steps that led to the triple-door entrance. There were six, and at the top he sat, dusted a place beside him, and waited until she joined him.

"Fountain of knowledge here," he said, jerking a thumb over his shoulder while his eyes never left the light traffic. "Great brains that will someday lead us all singing into the streets of a grand Utopia."

"You've had a bad week?" she said.

He grunted, shook his head as though the weight of the past five days had still not left him. "Not just that, Dale. It's everything. I've lost the old zing, the old enthusiasm for creating our future geniuses."

She smiled and watched a milk truck head ponderously for the highway two blocks to her right. "What you've lost, you see, is that fresh-from-college idealism that told you in dreams that you were going to change the world with your Mr. Chips brilliance."

"God, how true." He yanked his tie away from

his throat, snatched it off, and stuffed it into a jacket pocket. "Saturday, right? I was here all morning with a class of numbskulls who want prep school so badly their fathers can taste it. Freshmen, my dear lady, are the scourge of the universe. And despite Oxrun's high academic prowess, these monsters are no different. They aren't human, you know. None of them are. Willy . . . well, Willy and Jaimie and Melody and all the rest of those little kids put these dolts to shame with their questions and persistence."

"Why do you do it, then?" It was an old question they'd argued a hundred times, and she liked to think that perhaps it was her answers that kept him in teaching. But in her more sober moments she knew that wasn't the case. What kept him in teaching was the desire to stay in Oxrun Station. In addition to the lavish monies expended on contemporary equipment, book, experimental programs such as the one he ran each weekend morning, there was the town itself that affected him as much as it did her. It was more than home—a world unto itself, and though Vic wasn't village born, he was just as adamant of its qualities as any fifteenth-generation family.

"Why do I do it," he repeated solemnly. "How should I know? Stupid, I guess." He turned to her, and she was struck by the uncharacteristic lack of mischief that had always lurked beneath the surface of his expression. "Dale, would you like a partner in that joint of yours? Or a clerk? Or a push-the-broom-on-a-Saturday-afternoon boy? How about a shelf duster? Someone to keep Bella from attacking the kids and scaring them off? Maybe a sandwich man. You know the guys I mean—they walk up and down the streets with these boards publicizing the store and calling out the day's bargains. How about—''

''Hey, slow down,'' she said, and would have said more, but a patrol car cruised up to the curb and stopped. A voice called out and Vic slapped at his knees, touched her arm before descending to the sidewalk to talk with the driver.

It was time for her statement, she knew, and felt more guilty now because the shock of the boy's violent death had been sucessfully blunted by Vic's trying; and worse, she was more excited by the unusual inner change in her friend. They'd often joked about his work, her work, and somehow linking them in a purely professional way. But today she realized that Vic was serious—he wanted out, and into something less frantic, less awesomely responsible than the care and educational feeding of village youth. And what if she said no, what would he do? Leave the Station for the lure of the golden West, the metropolitan glamour of New York or Chicago, or the gambling dens of Las Vegas? What does an ex-teacher do, anyway, she wondered, and immediately pinched her wrist to distract herself. On top of what had happened less than two hours ago, this was too much and it wasn't true in the bargain. They were, these reflections and speculations, merely parts of a reaction, a grasping for something to take her mind off the tragedy, to dull her memory of the boy who only that morning had purchased a clipper ship he claimed he was going to complete on his own.

Like Jaimie McPherson and his mechanical monsters, Carl Booth and his intricate model cars; like Melody Forrester and her sewing, Carolyn and Debbie

Newcastle and their homemade dolls—all those children were like poor Willy: steady customers less than twelve years old who reached for the complex and somehow managed to achieve it. Questions that sometimes drove her mad, probing that once in a while frightened her. She wondered if they were all in the same class at school—that, she thought, would be a challenge for any teacher.

Little old men and women dressed up like children.

And yet, at the pond, they were frightened, crying, no pretense there of worldliness and false cynicism.

Kids, she thought, are interesting if you don't let them scare you half to death.

Vic straightened.

One of these days, she thought as he approached her, maybe I'll have a few of my own. One and one, and they'll be millionaires before I'm forty and will support me in the style to which I shall promptly become accustomed.

"What are you thinking so hard about?" he asked, reaching out a hand for her to take.

"Kids," she said without thinking. "And what mine will be like."

He held her hand a second longer as she stood. "Is that a proposal?"

Suddenly she realized what she'd been saying and fussed in her purse, her face down to hide a damning flush. "Of course not," she snapped. "Idle speculation."

"Oh well," he said, sighing loudly and searching the sky. "I guess there's always good old Liz Provence."

"Witch," she muttered.

"Nasty," he said.

"Sorry." She followed him to the sidewalk. "I guess, if she's a friend of yours, she can't be all that bad. I'm sorry, Vic. It's . . . it's the day."

"I know, don't worry about it. Hey," and he bent down suddenly and scooped a piece of paper from the concrete. "You dropped this."

She looked at the crumpled paper, blinked, and took it. "It's not mine." She unfolded it, read it, then looked at the patrol car speeding away. "Well," she said. "I've got a secret admirer."

# CHAPTER
# II

" 'Dear Miss Bartlett,' " she read as they left the high school behind them, " 'I know you like me and I like you so I want to see you today if you will let me. I will see you in the park cause that's where you always are and I will see you there because I want to say something to you. Please be in the park today so I can see you and tell you something.' " She handed the note to Vic and waited while he read it to himself. Silently. His eyebrows raised, his lips stiff to keep them from smiling.

"Well," he said to her unasked question, "it looks as though you've made a conquest, as they say. You been messing around with some of my boys, Dale?"

"You're being ridiculous," she said. "Besides, if you can't teach your classes any better English than this, they couldn't read the boxes in the store any-

23

way. I think it looks like a grade-school kid. Look at that printing, for crying out loud.''

"All right, all right, don't get excited. I was only kidding.''

"I'm not excited! Just curious. I wonder how long this was in my purse.''

"With all that garbage in it? Days, for all you know.''

She shook her head as she refolded the note and tucked it absently into her waistband. It couldn't have been there before today. Last night, while she was watching television, she had dumped the purse's contents onto the living room floor and finally separated the essentials from the empty gum wrappers, used tissues, and all the rest of the debris she'd picked up during the week. If the note had been there, she would have noticed it. It must have been while she was at the store. Her purse always sat on the counter next to the cash register. With people moving in and out throughout the morning, anyone could have slipped the paper in while she was in one of the four aisles with a customer.

"That's what you get for being so kind to them,'' Vic was saying. "Now that they know you're a sucker for their cute little smiles, they're trying . . . well, one of the little beasts is trying to put his grubby make on you, lady.'' He laughed at her expression and held up a palm to deflect her anger. "Come on, Dale, I'm only joking. But the printing, and that yellow-lined paper . . . it is one of your little ones, you know. Did you see anyone near you in the park before . . .'' He coughed, examined the sidewalk. "Before the accident?''

"No one but me," she said. "And the only time I left the purse alone . . ." She nodded quickly, once. "It could have been then, too. When I ran to see what all the commotion was, I left the purse, remember? God, an elephant could have come up without anyone seeing it."

"No," he said. "Only a lovesick one. Whoever that is," and he tapped her waist, "is mad for you, Miss Bartlett. What are you going to do about it?"

She didn't know, and for the moment it was inconsequential. They'd reached the Chancellor Avenue police station, another of the village's marble-and-granite imitations of a nonexistent Grecian temple, and she balked before allowing him to take her arm and lead her inside.

The first thing she saw was the low wooden railing that separated the waiting area from a large desk set up on a platform. The sergeant behind it looked up, recognized her, and immediately picked up one of the several telephones arrayed in front of him. Vic nodded to her and they sat on a smooth wooden bench against the wall, a faded picture of the Supreme Court hanging precariously above them. Dale had been in the station only twice before in her life, the last to speak to Chief Windsor about arranging for the return of her parents' coffins. Now the chief was dead, killed in a tragic fire at the Toal Mansion some time before, and she'd expected the place to be somehow different, changed. But it wasn't.

Behind the main desk on the rear wall were two frosted glass doors, their lettering indicating the detective and patrolman offices. A corridor interrupted the right-hand wall leading to the detention block, and a corridor off the left to the interrogation rooms and the chief's office. The ceiling was high, plaster, incongruously edged with dusty fat cherubs and unidentifiable flowers. Three hanging lamps encased in flat white globes dispensed a harsh light that added to the fading of the pale green walls. It could not have been anything else but a police station, she thought—it had that certain rushed, sweaty, intense odor about it even though crime in the village was anything but epidemic even in the worst of times.

Several patrolmen came in from the street, barely looking at her as they passed through the railing's gate, checked in with the sergeant, and vanished through the Detective Section door. Vic whistled softly the theme from "Dragnet," and she couldn't help a giggle before jabbing an elbow into his ribs. The door to the cell block opened, then, and a woman's voice blared obscenities at the back of a policewoman who immediately turned and blared them back. When she saw Dale gaping at her, she brushed lint from her shoulder, pushed at her short hair, and walked briskly outside.

"Oxrun's finest," Vic whispered. "Big-breasted, big-hipped, with the lungs of a stevedore."

"Cut it out, Vic," she said.

He snorted and leaned back, his head resting against the wall. She saw he was about ready to launch into a mocking and thoroughly accurate history of crime in Oxrun Station, was trying to think of a way to stop him, when Fred Borg came out of the left-hand corridor almost at a run. He headed for the desk, but when he spotted Dale and Vic, he veered and came through the gate. They stood immediately, and the two men shook hands.

"Fred, what's up?"

"What can I say, Vic? A million things going on at once. We got kids throwing late parties on the park hill after hours, complete with bonfires nobody sees until it's too late; we got a couple of women who got into a bottle-throwing argument at the Inn. And now we have this. Dale," he said, lowering his voice, "I'm sorry you had to wait, but Chief Stockton kept you here until the Campbells left, the back way. You can understand. She, Milly, is taking it remarkably well. Too calm, if you ask me, though. But Dave's already blaming the village for lack of supervision at the pond, the field, and anyplace else he can think of." The thin man wiped his brow with a sleeve and smiled wanly.

Not a policeman, she thought when he turned to call something to the desk sergeant. Even in the blue uniform he looks more like a priest or something.

"Come on," he said, taking her elbow. "Let's get this mess over with." But when Vic moved to accompany them, he motioned to the bench. "Really, Vic, unless you can say something a dozen others haven't already, I'd rather you'd stay out here, okay?"

When she looked, she saw a cloud darken the teacher's face, but it passed with a bravely false smile and a brisk nod.

"I'll be fine, honestly, Vic," she said. "Abe's not a monster, you know."

He said nothing, and she almost wished he could come with her. But Fred moved too quickly for her to react to the impulse, and they were soon walking down the corridor past the row of narrow benches that looked blindly up at a series of presidential portraits meticulously spaced on the opposite wall. All the seats were empty, and it could have been midnight for all the activity she'd seen, but there was no time left for comment. Fred knocked on an unlabeled door, opened it, and stepped inside.

"Smile," he whispered when she passed him, and despite her nervousness, she did.

The room was unexpectedly small, the white walls cluttered with photographs of Abraham Stockton shaking hands with men and women she didn't recognize, Abraham receiving awards and trophies, holding the hands of two of his four children. A solidly square desk centered the bare floor, and behind it a window with drawn green drapes. Stockton was standing by the only armchair in the room other than his own. He nodded, shook her hand without speaking, and retreated behind the desk to sit and shuffle papers. He was drawn, obviously tired, and his half century showed more than she'd noticed in the last dozen years. What was left of his red hair wisped behind his ears and made more prominent the large nose, jutted chin, the stubble of unshaven beard that divided his jaw from the loosely wattled neck. He pulled self-consciously at those folds now, and she waited patiently.

"Dale," he said at last, his voice only a husky memory of the basso that had made him so impressive when she was a child, "this is a rotten time to see you again."

"I know, Abe." She lifted her hand, dropped it

when there was nothing for it to do. "I don't know what to say."

"Yeah, I know. I just had Milly in here with Dave." He slammed a fist onto the desk. "I wish I wasn't the boy's godfather!" And just as suddenly as the explosion came, it vanished and he was as close to his official role as he could get at the moment. "Dale, I'll have to ask you what you saw, heard, anything at all. This will go into a report I'm making myself. And you'll probably have to repeat it at an inquest."

She glanced away from the eyes staring uncomfortably at her, concentrated on a monochrome print of racing greyhounds while she recited what she had done after hearing the first scream. Up to and including the moment Vic had taken her away to calm her down.

"Blake's a good man," Abe said, nodding. "My girl has him for history. I think she's in love with him."

"From what I hear, half the girls in the school are."

"Yeah. Well, listen, Dale, are you sure you haven't left anything out at all? You didn't stop on the way to call for help or something?"

She frowned, not in concentration but in puzzlement. "I don't understand, Abe. It happened just as I told you. Why? What's going on?"

Stockton dropped the folder he'd been holding and leaned back in his chair. Still he refused to meet her eyes. Instead, he picked up a pair of wire-rimmed glasses and perched them so the bridge was at the tip of his nose, looking over them at the door, through them at something noted on a pad by his hands.

"Dale, I'm not saying that you're not telling me the truth—"

"Well, of course I am, Abe. That's a terrible thing to imply here."

"—but it seems to me that there's a misstep in timing here. The pond's not all that big, as you know, and your running should have gotten you to the boy in time to pull him out. But you said he didn't respond to mouth-to-mouth, nor did he respond to anything the ambulance boys did, either." He scratched at his nose, rubbed the back of one hand along his neck. "Now, he did hit his head on something under the water. A rock, maybe. Stunned him, most likely. But though it doesn't take much more than a couple of drops, theoretically, to drown a man, drowning takes time, Dale. Willy shouldn't have drowned, even with that lump on his head. He shouldn't have. But he did."

She was confused now, and took a moment to search for something, anything that would dispel her bafflement. It was beyond belief that Abe would be trying, however diplomatically, to say that she somehow had a hand in Willy Campbell's death; it was also implausible and she said so, angrily, so frustrated she was ready to cry.

"Look, Dale, I know that!" he said without dropping his official pose. "Lord, I'm not saying you're a murderess—"

"Then why do you keep on about Willy not having time to drown. I mean, I didn't clobber him, if that's what you think. In fact, if you do you can ask the children. They'll tell you."

"Some children," he said sourly. "One says a green frog got him, another says the ducks. They all corroborate your story, there's no doubt there. But I was hoping, see, that you might have seen or heard something that would help me get rid of this itch I have in the back of my mind."

Dale stared down at her hands, saw them kneading her purse tightly. She willed them still, waited for them to relax before she looked up again. Abe was watching her now, openly and without a trace of suspicion. And the fact that she'd expected to see that suspicion rekindled her indignant anger. Carefully, forcing her breathing to steady itself, she returned his stare until he blinked once and rose, swept open the drapes, and turned his back to her, a shadow now in the brightening sunlit room.

"Dale, I'm ashamed of myself."

She wanted to say: *I should hope so*, bit the inside of her cheek to keep from speaking.

"Really ashamed. We're not exactly friends, but I've known you and your folks, bless them, for a long time." His hand drifted to the butt of his holstered revolver, rested there. "I'm not a big town cop, you know that, and I wasn't hired to be one, either. But I got this itch like I told you, and Dave Campbell's got one, too. He insists Willy could swim like those stupid ducks. Even if I let go, he isn't going to. I almost think he's scared, he's so insistent." Abe turned. "Dale, the fool's demanding an autopsy."

"My God, Abe, what's going on around here?"

He stepped around the desk and she saw the weary

resignation in his face. "I don't know, Dale. If I did, I'd be God, and I don't want that job, either." He held out his hand and she took it, was led to her feet and to the door which opened as soon as he rapped a knuckle on the glass. "Fred," he said to the waiting patrolman, "do me a favor and take Dale here . . . where? The store?"

"Forget it," she said, her smile only for Borg. "Vic's waiting. He can walk me the couple of blocks. Besides," she added as she moved into the corridor, "it wouldn't look very good, would it? I mean, little old me escorted around in a police car."

And without waiting for Abe's reply or Fred's company, she strode to the front and, with a brusque wave to Vic, nearly ran outside.

Whatever happened to that good day of mine, she thought. And when she could no longer take the stares, the whispers of an abrupt influx of browsing customers, she closed up the store. Mrs. Inness bustled out behind a flurry of solicitude, and the door was locked behind her, the shades drawn in the display windows, and the only illumination came from a small wine bottle lamp by the register. She sat on the high stool, shoulders slumped, hands restless in her lap. Vic had left her grudgingly after extracting a promise of a call later in the evening; but she had no intention of making it. Not even Vic and his mockery could drain the sack of righteous pain that had settled in her stomach.

She wanted to close her eyes, but she was afraid that Willy's image would rise ghostlike to haunt her waking hours; she wanted to call Chief Stockton and demand some sort of apology, extract a humbling admission of police error, but she admitted with great reluctance that he really couldn't have acted otherwise. It was—and she could think of no other word for it—humiliating. To be connected even for an instant with the possible murder of a little boy was more of a nightmare than anything she'd ever had as a child. But at the moment she had nothing but her own denials which she had, of necessity, kept to a minimum lest she thought to be protesting too much. To wait, then, was her only recourse, wait until the inquest and the results of that ridiculously demanded autopsy.

"Confound it, this isn't fair!" she said loudly.

A temptation surged to call the Campbells to see if they were harboring any suspicions, but the notion died instantly; they had their own sorrow, far worse than hers. She had met them as a pair only once, at an open house she'd held at the store two Halloweens ago. Milly was a dour, hard woman who reflected physically the hardships and sacrifices she'd made to bring her family over from the poverty of the Highlands; David was burly and quick-tempered, solemn most of the time, which made his smile all the more delightful. When he brought his carvings to the store to be sold, she made it a game to make him grin. A superstition: to part his lips would mean a good sales day; and she'd never spoiled it by counting the receipts. There were four, she recalled, in the Campbell household: Dave, Milly, Will, and an aunt—father's or mother's she never knew. They lived somewhere on Chancellor Avenue, her street, beyond the park where the houses were few, old and poor introductions to the estates that followed. Campbell's woodwork—chessmen, statuettes, intricate children's toys—seemed to be their only source of income, but the prices she was able to ask, and the prices she always received, were probably more than enough to keep them going; at least, she'd never heard Willy complain of hunger, nor had to endure Dave's grumblings about bills past due.

No, she thought, calling them was out. She only had to wait, and stop herself from seeing damning accusations each time someone looked at her without a smile. That, she decided, would be easier said than done; the people who had come in that afternoon only wanted to see the woman who'd discovered the body, to cluck their ghoulish sympathy and depart with some unimaginable dollop of gossip.

In a deliberate attempt to sidetrack her mind, to find something less morbid to dwell on, she wandered the aisles, straightening a box here, a carton there, finger-dusting a doll and poking a stuffed animal. And then she began to wonder about the note in her purse. It made little difference how it had gotten there; what she wanted to know was who its author was. She grinned and allowed a short laugh to keep her company. Vic was probably right; it was a love note, most likely from one of the many children who came regularly to the store, if only to talk to her because she was more than willing to spend time with them. Obviously, one of the boys had developed a crush, much as he would for a favorite teacher or pretty young librarian. In a way, she thought, it was rather flattering, and she scolded herself for actually preening at the idea. But in a quite different sense, it would be a difficult matter to deal with. She'd have to locate her secret admirer somehow and try to ease him down from the cloud he was riding.

Let him down gently.

She laughed, loudly and long this time, tears welling and brushed away with the back of a hand. How often had she been forced by circumstance to perform that delicate operation on men her own age? She tried counting, could not. Ever since the store came into her hands, and her hands became eager, she had been too busy, and too many of the men who sought more than her temporary company were too bluntly hostile toward the idea of maintaining a business other than their own. It was, however, an unalterable condition of whatever future plans in matrimony she might make. To sell the store—now or ever—was unthinkable, would have been unforgivable.

"Love me, love my toys," she said as she checked the rear door lock and set the burglar-alarm systems. "Take me, you fool, I'm yours, but you'll have to take my dollies, too."

By the time she had slipped into a light cardigan and grabbed her purse, hints of good humor had flushed her cheeks, dispersed the clouds that the sky hadn't seen. She tested the doorknob, turned away from the store, and headed left down the street. Shadows were already crawling toward her as the sun set slowly toward eight o'clock. Only one car passed her. She was amazed at the time, had to blink and stare closely at a clock in a jewelry store to be sure she wasn't seeing things. She'd been alone three hours after Bella had left, then, three hours that she would have sworn were only a dreadfully slow-moving one.

It was two blocks to Chancellor, a left turn and a brisk walk across Park Street and Western to reach the corner house her parents had left her. Traffic moved slowly by in both directions: west for those heading for the highway and the entertainments to be found in the larger towns some distance away; east for the inevitable Saturday-night parties that seemed integral to the affluent life for which Oxrun was known among those who knew she existed.

The house was smaller than its neighbors, a simple Cape Cod with a narrow front porch and an abundance of trees that made the structure seem twice as small. She stood on the top step and stared across the street to the high iron fence of the park's perimeter. Had she the miracle ability, she could have seen through the closely spaced trees straight to the lower, western tip of the pond; and indeed, during the late winter, she was able to make out the gaily dressed skaters when the light was bright in early afternoon.

Now there was nothing but green and the shadows therein, and as she turned to fit her key into the front lock, she wondered who it was she would have met had she gone to the pond and waited. Nobody, probably, she thought. If Willy's death hadn't frightened them off, the sheer boldness of her response probably would have.

Another one missed, Mom, she thought, but I don't think I'm quite that desperate yet.

The foyer was small, barely large enough to hold a side table on the left, coat rack with an oval mirror set into its back on the right. She dropped purse and sweater onto the table and shuffled into the living room where she kicked off her shoes and turned on the television, two movements habitual, nearly ritual. Then on into the dining room and, behind that, the kitchen where her kettle was waiting. Too tired to contemplate cooking a complete meal, she grabbed a frozen dinner from the refrigerator and tossed it noisily into the oven. Back through the foyer, then, and into the sitting room on the right which she had turned into a greenhouse experiment. Dozens of plants from violets to ivy on shelves, hanging in multicolored bowls from the ceiling, propped precariously on the front and side window sills. The air here was perceptively sharper, and as she drifted from one plant to another with mister in hand, she spoke to them, cuddled them, tsked and scolded. Originally, there had been three rooms on this side of the house: the sitting room (the living room is for company, her mother had decreed) and two bedrooms. When Dale moved in to stay, she'd knocked out one wall to enlarge the room for her plants, designated the back bedroom a study where, because of her upbringing, she had planned to put her books and TV. That worked for only a few months, however, when she decided that to walk all that way just to sit down and relax was ridiculous. The change, then, and the greatest adjustment to being alone.

She also felt safer with the bulk of the house behind her.

When the plants were done and settled, she hurried upstairs to shower and change into jeans and a man's white shirt which she tied just beneath her breasts.

Then she ran down again to take out her dinner and slump on the couch in front of the television.

It was dark.

Cooling.

She dumped the aluminum tray into a wastebasket and was searching through the program guide for something more than situation comedies when the doorbell rang.

"Not now, Vic!" she muttered, yanking the shirt's knot open and tucking the material into her jeans. A quick look in the foyer mirror and she opened the door, caustic quip ready. She swallowed it.

"Miss Bartlett?"

The porch light was off, and the tiny figure on the welcome mat could easily have been a child were it not for the almost theatrical cackling in the aged, high voice.

"You are Dale Bartlett, aren't you? Have I the correct house, then?"

Dale quickly brushed a hand over her face and smiled, stepped aside and watched amusedly as the little figure scuttled into the living room without invitation and faintly climbed onto the armchair next to the couch.

Eighty, Dale thought as she took her place on the sofa; a year's salary she's no younger than that.

The old woman was wearing a heavy dark overcoat and black scarf, the combination of which making her gray-white face all the more stark, her heavy black eyebrows all the more out of place. There was no use of cosmetics that Dale could see other than a patting of rouge on the flattened, hollow cheeks. And when she smiled, most of her teeth were stained yellow or dark brown.

And she was so small, her feet in their heavy black shoes were unable to touch the floor when she sat back.

"I'm Flora Campbell," she said, nodding just so while bone-thin fingers fumbled with her coat, opening it to her waist. "Willy's aunt."

Dale could only stare. Phrases, trite and well-intentioned, jumbled her into stunned silence. The woman knew her discomfort and smiled again.

"My David tells me you were the one who found little Will in the pond."

"I . . . was," she said, her throat constricting and suddenly gone dry.

The woman lifted a hand and yanked the scarf from her head. Her hair, waist-long, was a shimmering white so youthfully gleaming Dale was unable to stifle a gasp. A smile. And suddenly she relaxed.

"You can tell an old woman a lot of things," Flora Campbell said, "but she seldom believes it until she sees it. I see you. And I'm here to tell you, young woman, that there'll be none of us who blame you for what happened today. None of us."

"Miss . . . Mrs. . . ."

"Flora, please. I've never married, and I think Miss is a little too much for a hag my age."

Dale nodded eagerly. "Flora. Thanks. And thank you for coming out tonight. I was really beginning to think Mr. Campbell was going to get the police after me or something. I mean, even the chief—"

"Abraham is a good boy, Miss Bartlett, and he does what he has to. David says do this and that, and

Abraham must do this and that because David is the father of the boy. But David takes his grief in different ways. He doesn't like to believe in things like accidents. He demands a cause, you see. Always a cause.''

Suddenly mindful of her role, Dale moved to stand. ''Flora, would you like a cup of tea, or some water? It must be a long walk from your house to here. I'm sorry, but you startled me for a moment and I'm forgetting myself.''

''Relax, child,'' the old woman said, waving her down again. ''Relax, I'm not going to bite you, you know. I just thought you should know what it is we're thinking back home.''

Dale looked down to her lap, to her hands twisting mindlessly. ''I appreciate that, Miss Campbell, I really do. It's awfully kind of you.''

''You knew my Will?''

She looked up quickly. Flora had leaned forward in the chair, shrinking her still further. Had it not been for the summer blue eyes and the incredible hair, Dale would have thought she was speaking with a corpse, or a Halloween-costumed youngster. ''I knew him, yes, but not all that well. He came into the store to buy models once in a while, and with his friends. He bought ships, planes, things like that. Especially ships, though. He liked ships of all kinds.''

''A sailor. He wanted to be a sailor,'' Flora said, her eyes roving the ceiling. ''He spent much of his time in his room doing those things. The walls are full, and his mother always said she was going to throw them out. Of course, I wouldn't allow that, but she said it often.'' She straightened, crossed her ankles. "Did you see him today? Before, is what I mean. Did you see him before he went to the park?" Then a finger went up before Dale could answer. "I'm sorry for the questions, young woman, but understand that I'd like to know what it was he was doing today. His mother, too, and my David. It helps sometimes, you see."

Dale wasn't sure she saw at all, but if this is what the family wanted then she wasn't going to be the one to deny them. She explained what had happened in the store with the clipper ship and Mrs. Inness, and the joke the boy had tried to make with Bella's favorite phrase. It wasn't long in the telling, but she noticed the old woman's lips moving as if trying to memorize the conversation, to recall it verbatim for the boy's bereft parents.

"Did he not give you anything, then? A present or something of the like?"

Dale inexplicably remembered the figurine in the boy's hand, but saw no need to mention that here. The police, in fact, had most likely already returned it. "No, of course not," she said. "I'm not really in the habit of accepting gifts from my customers, Miss Campbell."

The woman waved her hands apologetically in front of her. "No, no, I didn't mean it like that. But Will was that kind of a boy, Miss Bartlett. He liked many people and always wanted to be giving them things. Like his father's work, for instance. After the poor man works so hard on them for hours, Will . . . Will, the poor wee boy, would take something that struck his fancy and give it to someone he liked. Like you, Miss Bartlett, I'm sure."

"Well," Dale said, "I'm sorry but he's never given me anything but a smile and a few bright moments during my day."

She didn't know why she'd said exactly that, but they seemed to be the right words for the moment. Flora caught her breath, released it in a sigh that lowered her gaze to the carpet for several long seconds. Then, without preamble, she pushed herself from the chair and was already in the foyer before Dale could recover and catch up with her.

"Are you sure you wouldn't like a drink of something before you go, Miss Campbell? I don't have a car or I'd offer you a lift home. Perhaps I could call a cab?"

"No, it's all right, dear. You've given me quite enough already."

Dale opened the door, walked across the porch as Flora climbed haltingly down the steps to the walk. Her hair was covered again, blended into the dark of her coat, and she was a shadow in the street before she reached the corner. Dale waved, not sure she was seen, then sat heavily on the top step.

To the east as far as she could see, the black wall of the park shadows seemed an almost tangible barrier. A car sped past in the wake of its headlights, its engine abrasive in the silence of the street. A mockingbird dropped from the huge maple in the front yard and soared over the house. One of these years, she thought, I'm going to put in a hedge or some fencing. The small lawn was already beginning to look worn and August-tired from the children who passed each day and used it for a wrestling mat on their way to and from school.

She waited, then, for the relief to come, the lifting of the weight that her imaginary guilt had grown, the lifting caused by the dispensation of the strange old woman.

She waited, and there was nothing.

Only an odd sense of coming in on the middle of a film without knowing the plot. Ordinarily she would have thought nothing of Miss Campbell's visit, but she realized in dismay that suspicion was fast becoming an active part of her nature; after all, the Campbells live a good two miles down the road—was it natural such an ancient creature should walk all that way to deliver a message she could have given over the telephone? On the other hand, perhaps she believed in the personal touch, that the words would seem more potent, and more sincere.

Then: on what other hand, she thought—what am I talking about?

She stood.

Good night, Willy Campbell, she said to the trees whispering to themselves in the park across the street. I hope you're still laughing.

# CHAPTER
# III

June.

July.

Summer settled in with an enervating vengeance, a furnaced revenge for the respite of winter. Lawn sprinklers worked hourly, vainly, more use to the children who ran through them than the grass they watered. Cars moved sluggishly, pedestrians as though gravity had multiplied—and when it showered, there was a rising of steam from tarmac streets. Breezes became treasures, clouds good omens, and the air-conditioned stores were palaces from which few dared or desired to venture toward home.

With no holidays in sight, Dale left the store in Mrs. Inness' eager care and took a week off to paint the kitchen, rearrange the living room, tend her plants, and spend most of the late afternoons wandering through the shade of the park trees hoping to stumble across a lost plane ticket to somewhere in Alaska. By the end of the month and the last day free of Bella's complaining, she was bored. She wished she had taken Vic's halfhearted advice and found a resort someplace a thousand miles away, with beaches and breakers and tall cool drinks brought to her poolside lounge by white-coated valets. It would have been a change. A needed one, she thought; but she hadn't taken a vacation since her first year, when Bella had seized the opportunity to turn the store around to what it had been. By staying close to home, she told herself, she could pass by on accidental occasion and sneak a look inside to see that all was well. And whenever she did, there was Bella, glaring back at her and shaking her head, pointing a finger, mouthing a *go away* behind a not entirely sincere laugh.

She dined with Vic often, saw a few of her acquaintances when she felt like it, but generally shunned those who might bring up the misery of Willy Campbell's inquest. It had gone by fast enough, perfunctory and official, with the verdict expected and unprotested. But the sight of Dave and Milly Campbell sitting in the front row as she retold her story had been unnerving enough to put her to bed for the rest of the day. Dave had been pale, his great frame collapsed in defeat like a pricked balloon, and from Milly only an unconcerned stare as if she didn't much care.

The children still came to the store, Jaimie and Carl quietly vying for the leadership Willy had had.

For Willy was now a poignant memory. Even Bella seemed distressed for a while that he wasn't around to poke fun at her greeting.

It grew hotter.

It became August.

On a Saturday afternoon, Dale broke out of the oven her house had become and entered the park. The playing field was generally flat, but the east end rose to a gentle hill crowned thickly with pine and maple, a hill that served adequately for a long view of the bandstand halfway down, the field, the tops of the buildings in Oxrun's center. With a thermos of cold tea nestled against her side, she stretched out on the warm grass and cupped her hands behind her head. Heat hazed the sky and bleached the gold of the sun. She closed her eyes finally to the buzzing of invisible insects.

She wanted to think, to have a talk with herself about the evening before when Vic had taken her to the Chancellor Inn for a meal and a drink and a night of sweated frantic dancing; and after he had kissed her, standing on the bottom step of the porch, he had proposed. Awkwardly, shyly, he had taken her so by surprise that she'd demurred like some coy southern belle urging her man to wait until the war was over and he was home to stay. He'd taken it well, joked about it as he walked hurriedly back to his rust-streaked car; but there was a slump at his shoulders she'd never seen before, and pity had almost driven her to scream out an acceptance. He had gone, though, before the impulse had peaked, and she had slept badly. Weakly blaming it on the heat.

A shout from below, and she raised her head to see wildly cheering boys surrounding one of their fellows at home plate. A home run, she thought and applauded the feat silently before closing her eyes again.

Listening to the faint laughter.

Drifting.

Listening to the drone of a bee that hovered by her cheek, then sped off without lighting.

Listening to the rustle of her red print blouse as she took a deep breath and lifted her breasts, exhaled, and felt their weight pushing her further into the ground.

Drifting.

Dozing.

*She was walking. Looking down. On water. Brown and deep and splotched below the surface with a green that had never seen the sun. Looking up. There was no shore. Only water, brown water that lay calm beneath a sky that rippled over invisible stars like a stream over pebbles.*

*A pace, and the water didn't move beneath her. Another, and a dragonfly as big as her fist exploded from nowhere to bump against her arm. She cried out, grabbed her forearm and saw the abrasion raising welts that bled, slowly. A drop at a time.*

Another cheer. A breeze that moved the leaves above her to cast dappled shadows over her face. Spots, then, of cool and warm, and she turned her cheek onto the grass while one hand deserted the pillow and rested on her stomach.

*Several yards ahead of her the brown water cleared. Still walking, not thinking of how she was staying afloat, she approached the uneven circle and looked down again. Bubbles. Small, rising, breaking through the surface and splashing into her face. A fetid stench*

*jerked her face away, a stench that took on color as
it drifted upward and waited. The color was brown,
laced with green and purple and tendrils of white.
The bubbles came faster, broke more violently, sent
her scurrying to escape the odor that wrenched a
gagging cough from her throat. The color hovered,
coalesced, became a cloud that grew, whirling within
itself and bobbing over the clear calm water.*

Her fingers gripped satin fabric and pulled convul-
sively. Slowly the blouse worked out from her jeans,
exposing her midriff, which grew hot instantly and
beaded perspiration that ran down her side. Her lips
opened, gulped, and her tongue flicked snakelike
over them, leaving them dry. She swallowed, tossed
her head to the other cheek and her freed hand joined
the other. Within seconds her blouse was completely
undone and one finger toyed with the bottom button.

*The cloud rose as the bubbles fed it, rose and lost
the green and the purple and the tendrils of white,
replaced them with red and gold and great lances of
black. All of it swirling, all of it contained within the
stench that was brown, the stench that spread over
the water and trapped her, forced her to her knees.
She crawled; and suddenly, looking back over her
shoulder at the cloud big as she, felt moisture on her
bare feet. She was sinking. With every move another
fraction of an inch. Hands to her knees she fought
the pressure of the stench that downed her, and
searched the level horizon for signs of land. A step,
and she sank. A step, and she sank and began to cry
when she realized she could not stop walking.*

An ant with its partner scuttled over her forehead.

She brushed at them, whimpered, rolled over onto her stomach.

*She called out names, all the names she had known, but there was no one; and the bubbles were larger and the cloud was moving toward her and she was in the water to her knees and sinking faster. To her thighs, her shoulders, her neck, and the cloud hovered over her. She looked up, heard a voice. Whispering. Muttering. Murmuring. Words that made no sense in a language that had no meaning. And as the water reached her mouth and spilled acidly through her clenched lips, she saw a face smiling at her, nodding, covered with blades of drenched grass that dripped red slime and blinded her eyes.*

*Willy!*

"Willy!" and she sat up, shaking, hugging herself as she looked around quickly. She slapped at her forehead where the ants had been, then shoved knuckles against her eyelids until she gasped in pain.

"Brother," she whispered, glanced guiltily down the slope. But her cry hadn't been noticed. The game continued, the couples with their picnics and their children still settled around the bandstand waiting for the suppertime concert.

Freud, she thought as she grabbed a nearby trunk and hauled herself up, you'd have a field day with me, that's for sure.

She snatched a handkerchief from her hip pocket and wiped the perspiration from her arms and face, shuddering at the afterimage of the horror that had blinded her in the dream. Without thinking, she tossed the cloth away and moved carefully back through the trees to the path she'd taken to the top of the hill. As she crossed the low summit she passed through a small clearing obviously widened by hand. A large blackened patch in its center reminded her of Fred's complaint: the kids were evidently still holding their night-based parties, and she wished for a moment they would never be caught. Beer, hot dogs, awkward gropings in the lessons of sex—it was a time they shouldn't be denied and she had a feeling, a good one, that Fred wasn't trying all that hard.

There was no one else walking this deep in the park, and as soon as she found a bench she took it and held her head in her hands until dizziness passed and the world returned.

Yet it wasn't the dream itself that had frightened her but the fact that it was an apparent culmination of fragmentary nightmares that had been building over the past several weeks. The water had been there, and the walking, and the bubbles rising from that clear patch in the brown. But fragments only, half remembered and soon forgotten shortly after she awakened.

Why now, she wondered. Why now and here and not home in bed? And why little Willy in that cloud two months after the funeral? It couldn't be residual guilt; there was no guilt at all as far as she was concerned. Both Dave's ancient aunt, and even Stockton, had assured her there was nothing more she could have done. No guilt, then. But . . . what?

She wiped a sleeve under her nose, tucked in her blouse, and began the meandering descent. She reached one of the refreshment kiosks in the middle of a circular tarmac island and finished three tall colas before her change ran out. Further, and she was abreast of the games and heard more clearly the shouts of the teams. A hundred yards more and she'd be at the entrance, but she felt too nervous to go home just yet, and definitely not up to a sneak look into the store. When she reached the sidewalk, then, she still hadn't made up her mind which direction to take. The library, cool and silent, was a possibility dismissed at the thought of meeting Nat Clayton, the head librarian, who kept the building open late on Saturdays for those who worked all week. Dale didn't think she'd be able to stop herself from relating her dream; and though she was friendly and not much older, Mrs. Clayton just didn't know her well enough to understand the fear that still clung to her shoulders in this broad August daylight.

A drink, she thought, and smiled, startling a woman and her husband as they passed her. A drink would be nice, but the Chancellor Inn was too far to walk. Only four blocks over and two down, but in Oxrun the blocks were nearly twice normal length and that she was definitely not up to managing just yet.

"For crying out loud, sit on the curb and wait to get run over," she told herself, and smiled more broadly when the couple snapped their heads around. "Nice day," she called, tossing her head, running her fingers through her hair. The couple only hurried away.

"The same to you, folks," she muttered, then glanced straight ahead to where High ran into Park and saw Vic rounding the far corner and heading directly for her. There was no hesitation. She yelled, raised both arms and yelled again until he looked up and saw her. When he broke into a run, she dashed across the street to meet him, threw both arms around his waist, and lifted her face to be kissed.

"Very nice," he said when she released him. "Is this a yes, or is it my sexual karma that made you so wanton in the middle of the day?"

"Don't flatter yourself," she laughed.

"What would Mrs. Inness say to such a display, Miss Bartlett? You'll give the poor thing a massive heart attack."

"Nuts to that old bag," she said, taking his hand and pulling him back the way he'd come. They passed the grade school and she glanced nervously up at the blank shaded windows. "I've got to tell you about a dream I've just had."

"Oh, you too?"

She stopped suddenly and moved to stand in front of him. "What do you mean, me too?"

He was startled by her vehemence, but recovered rapidly enough to retake her arm and move her along. "I mean, my dear, that I too have just been through a dream. A nightmare, actually. You see, I've just been to the Board office this beautiful Saturday afternoon—the poor devils work hard at the end of August. I wanted to see what could be done about getting some new programmed learning books I wanted for my honors course this year. Well, it seems they won't be getting me the book, or anything else for that matter." He bowed and gave her a sardonic grin. "This model teacher, shop lady, has been given the old proverbial pink slip."

"You want a job?" was the first thing she thought of to say, flippant, and she regretted it instantly. He only smiled, however, and turned her at the corner into the luncheonette. Most of the stools at the white-and-pink counter were taken, as were the dozen booths that stretched along the sidewalk side back toward the kitchen. They found one, however, hidden behind a paperback book rack and, after snaring a waitress, slid in. Vic set an ashtray between them, lighted a cigarette for himself when Dale declined. He stared mutely at the smoke curling blandly toward the ceiling.

"You asked, madam, if I wished gainful employment."

"Come on, Vic, I'm sorry. I wasn't thinking. It was a poor joke. I'm sorry."

"On the contrary," he said, still watching the smoke. "If you are serious, then so am I. Assuming, of course, that you are speaking about that den of sinful fun you laughingly call a toy store." His grin became wry. "The . . . other matter is obviously now postponed. A slight change in plans, you might say."

She watched him reach up to pull at his beard, stroke his mustache, then took his wrist and settled his hand over hers on the table between them. "Don't do that," she said softly. "I know it means you're nervous. Don't be. You don't have to be, Vic, not around me."

"Well, how do you think I feel!"

She took the verbal slap and excused it. There was little of the confidence of expertise about him now, and she wanted to hold him, put his head to her chest and say stupid things that would promise them the moon and realize nothing. That, she knew, was precisely what he didn't need that moment. And her own fear born of the dream was shunted aside before she could think twice about it.

She waited until their coffee arrived, the creamer and sugar bowl scrounged from another booth, then said, "Why you, and why so late before telling you? I don't understand."

"If I did, fully, I could bottle it and be a millionaire," he said. "What I was told was this: although my classroom deportment and instruction is reasonably above reproach, my other activities have made it clear to the Board that I was not in full and complete comprehension of my contractual obligations."

"Now what is that supposed to mean?"

"When I asked the good old Treasurer of the Board, Harmon Randolph Blanchard, that very same question, he said—and this was man to man, mind you—he said that I was supposed to be teaching high school students, not taking jobs away from the grade-school faculty."

Dale put a finger to her forehead and scratched, shaking her head.

"Wait and patience, love, and it will become clear. I hope. I'm still working on it myself. I tried to get more from him but couldn't, so I set my gorgeous bulk down on his secretary's desk and wheedled and pleaded in my best sloe-eyed manner until she told me in the strictest confidence that the grade-school faculty was—and how well she put it for a college graduate—disturbed because several students were getting too far ahead of their regular class. It seems these same few geniuses, which is a loose word because they are not geniuses, were the ones like Will Campbell and Melody and Jaimie McPherson who come over to the high school to mess around with the older kids. The idea is, see, that since I am in charge of the yard and since I talk with those kids a great deal, I must be tutoring them on the sly. This would not only be in violation of my contract but also in violation of the agreement made between Board and Teachers' Association. It also makes the grade-school people look stupid. Ergo, some fat-headed building representative complained to the grade-school principal, who complained to my principal, who, since this is my tenure year, saw fit not to mention it to me but rather nipped in the bud my revolutionary tactics by terminating my contract.''

"But, Vic, he can't do that!''

"Oh, but technically he can do just that. They bought me off.''

Dale frowned.

"What I mean is, when I threatened suitable bodily harm and loss of other goodies through a massive and publicity-seeking legal action, they promised to give me my full year's salary just to keep me quiet. And I took it.''

"Now that's stupid of you, Vic,'' she snapped, slapping cup to saucer so hard her coffee slopped over onto the table. "What about your ideals? Your wanting to teach those kids? What happened to your principles?''

"With great self-control I will pass over the obvious puns and simply state that principles do not put bread on my humble table, my love. Besides,'' and his voice lost his sarcasm, "after this, I couldn't work for that simple-minded jackass anyway. I'm not a gadfly. It wouldn't work. And neither am I brave enough to be a martyr that I'd run with my cause, no matter how just in this case, to the papers and anyone who would listen. I stuck them for all the money they would have paid me anyway, and I ran. Simple as that. I was on my way to your place to tell you about it when"—and he grinned—"we met so delightfully."

She wanted to comment, but there was too much to be said. He saw the struggle in her face and took her hand, held it tightly while the luncheonette filled, emptied, filled and became noisy, and the waitress hovered to either clear the table or take their order. Not looking up, Vic asked for the day's specialty for the two of them. Alone again, her hand still in his, she wondered just who first thought there was some sort of impartial justice floating around the universe; it was an insane notion with no bearing at all on the way life at its most real functioned. But when she said so, angrily and with tears stinging to make her blink rapidly, he shook his head.

"Poor attitude, Dale."

"Well, what am I supposed to think, Vic? It just isn't fair!"

"Nothing is, and when you get used to it, things like this pass."

"But what are you going to do?"

"You said you wanted to give me a job—temporarily, until I can find something more substantial?"

"Yes," she said, and couldn't help a sly grin when she pictured Mrs. Inness' face when he walked in with her Monday morning. "But you've got to promise me something."

"Anything, boss," he said, saluting.

"No seductions in the storeroom. I have an image, you know."

"My Lord, such a mouth on such a beautiful woman," he said, laughing. "You are going to have to change your ways."

Arrival of the meal silenced them, and Dale used the time to mull over what she had heard and what she had just done. It would be interesting, she thought, to discover exactly who the complainer had been and how it was discovered that Vic had been the one talking to the children when they visited the high school. But despite his anger over what had happened, he'd given no signals of wanting revenge and she abandoned the idea, replacing it with another: a brief examination complete with surreptitious glances at Vic of her violent reaction to his news. It wasn't merely sympathy for a friend's misery—empathy was more like it; and friend, she realized, wasn't the word for the situation or the relationship—now she was his boss and, she thought, a beautiful situation that was going to be.

"Hey," he said, lifting a spoon and pointing over her shoulder, "isn't that the old Campbell woman over there?"

Dale turned in time to see Dave and his aunt walk into the luncheonette. She ducked away but not quickly enough. While Dave spoke to the counterman, his aunt remained oblivious to the stares she received and came over to the booth.

"Flora," Dale said, "what brings you here?" She nodded toward her plate. "It can't be because of the cuisine."

The old woman laughed appreciatively. She was

dressed as Dale had seen her the night of her visit, yet despite the temperature there was no sign of perspiration anywhere on her face. "David takes me in once a month to do me some shopping," she said. "I am very much in love with the jewelry in the windows, you see." She spread her hands. "Not that I can purchase the pieces that I like, but it pleases me to look just the same. And how have you been, Miss Bartlett?"

"Well, and awfully hot. I don't know how you can take that coat in such miserable weather."

Flora smiled and touched the black buttons carefully. "It serves me to wear it, no matter the weather. I suppose you might say my blood is cold, still tuned to the winters across the water."

"Miss Campbell," Vic began, but she quickly waved him silent.

"I must run now. Do be careful, Miss Bartlett," she said, "and sleep well in this terrible heat."

Without waiting for reply, she returned to Dave and the two of them walked out to the street, not looking back.

"Friendly, isn't she?"

Dale shrugged. "Interesting, more likely."

"You're telling me? You notice how she falls in and out of that Highland burr? It's as though she can't decide whether or not to use it. She must be near a hundred years old."

"Eighty," Dale said, "so Willy once mentioned."

"Well, she likes you, obviously. What did you do, take a thorn from her paw?"

"Vic, that's not fair," and she explained about Flora's walk to her house and the absolution she'd brought. Vic thought it a splendid gesture, though he wondered aloud why neither of the parents had made a follow-up visit. Dale didn't know, and she didn't care. What was done was over, and at the moment she had more important things to worry about.

"Aha," he said. "Such as?"

"Such as catching Mrs. Inness before she leaves for the night. I was going to spring you on her first thing Monday, but now I don't think that's a good idea. She might keel over from the shock."

"Am I so impressive?"

Dale laughed, more like a bark, and hurried him through his dessert so fast he belched all the way down the street to the shop where Mrs. Inness was just preparing to shoo out the few remaining boys clustered around a display of metal soldiers. When Dale and Vic walked in, she left the boys and planted herself behind the counter, officiously slapping a hand on a receipt pad.

"Dale," she said stiffly, "I'm glad you've come. You've saved me a trip out your way."

Dale saw the color drained from the woman's cheeks, leaving her dabs of rouge and lipstick a brilliant and unpleasant contrast to the curled mass of gray hair piled atop her great head. Another crisis, she thought wearily, and leaned against the counter, smiling, waving once to a passer-by before making a show of scanning the store as though searching for something dreadfully amiss. The smile became a strain, then, and Vic deserted her for a wandering through the aisles.

"Dale, are you listening to me?"

"What?" She jerked her head around and leaned

her chin on a palm, looked up with the smile gone. "I'm sorry, Bella. What's wrong? Are you feeling all right?"

"I'm feeling just fine, thank you, and please do not try to change the subject."

"Then what is it? Something wrong with the store?"

Again she looked around, then back with a carefully blank expression.

"There is nothing wrong with the store, either. You entrusted the sales to me and I believe I handled myself adequately. What is wrong, however, is that I am going to have to tender my resignation, effective tonight."

Dale jerked straight, hurried around the counter, and climbed the platform on which it rested. She stood between Bella and the display window and folded her arms over her chest. "What do you mean, you're quitting? Come on, Bella, what's wrong?"

Mrs. Inness pulled a lace-edged handkerchief from her neckline and patted her jowls, her cheeks, pursed her lips and patted them. Daintily and, Dale thought unkindly, grotesquely. "What is wrong, Dale, is those incorrigible children. Ever since you left they've been coming in here to persecute me."

"Bella, for God's sake, they love you! They get a little rough at times, I admit—"

"They have been downright cruel to me, Dale, and I won't stand for it. They ask me questions, all kinds of questions that I can't possibly answer. I tell them to go to the library and they say the librarian won't let them in the grown-up sections where they could use the adult dictionaries and encyclopedias. But they keep at me! All the time! And then they stand in the corners, fingering the dolls and what have you, whispering just loud enough for me to hear them.'' Her face tightened, and Dale dropped her arms when she saw the shimmer of tears. "I've never told you this before, Dale, but they do this all the time. And . . . they make fun of me, of my weight and the way I dress and the way I talk. When you were gone they didn't have your unthinking friendship to hid behind. They . . . they were . . .'' She tossed her head and swallowed. "Vicious. That's the only word. Vicious.''

"Bella, please.'' She lay a gentle hand on the woman's shoulder. "Kids don't know about things like the social graces, Bella. Whatever is silly they think is funny, and if they think they can get away with something, they will and as often as they can. It's not deliberate cruelty. Look at Willy and the way he used to tease you about saying 'May I assist you, young man' all the time. It wasn't because he didn't like you—''

"Easy for you to say.''

"—but because he just didn't know any better.''

Bella slumped onto the stool and folded her hands wordlessly over the pad. The boys had come up to the counter with their purchases, and she worked at smiling while taking their money and thanking them when they refused the bags she'd pulled off the shelf at her knees. When the door closed, she wrote out the receipt and speared it on the nail driven into the wood by the register.

"Now,'' Dale said, "are you going to tell me that's the last sale you're ever going to make in here?''

Bella only dabbed at her cheeks again.

"You know, you're always invoking my parents at me. I could do the same to you. They trusted you, Bella, and if nothing else they taught me that I need you in here." A sag appeared in Bella's stiffly set spine. "Especially now."

"Oh? Why now?"

Dale rubbed a hand over her face to hide the grin, put her back to the counter and slumped in a posture of conspiracy. "Victor Blake. He was fired today from the high school faculty, you know."

"You must be joking, Dale!"

"I'm not. He's been rather good to me since I've known him, you know, and he was the first one . . ." She took a deep breath, not wanting to say it. "He was the first one to reach me that day in June when Willy drowned. I . . . I promised him a job, Bella, to help him until something else comes along. I'm going to need you to help me show him the ropes. You know how busy it's going to get in here with school opening up next week, and the Christmas and Halloween seasons sneaking up on us again. I just can't handle it all without you."

"I will do it if you promise me something," Bella said.

"What do you need, a raise?"

She pulled away suddenly, her face now a mask of indignation. "Certainly not! That would be blackmail, or something of the sort. I want you to promise me you'll have a talk with those . . . children. Get them . . . well, get them to watch their language while they're in here. Especially that Jaimie person."

"Jaimie? Jaimie McPherson?" Vic said, coming

up so silently that neither of the women heard him. Bella made to leave, but Dale held her hand and explained to Vic what Jaimie, Carl, and the others had been doing while she'd been gone. Vic, at once angry and solicitous, impulsively covered Bella's free hand with his own. "Mrs. Inness," he said solemnly, "I think I'll make this my first task on the job. Jaimie is too smart for his own good. He and Melody and those Newcastle brats. I'll be sure that they'll be on their best behavior when they're in here. I promise you that."

"You're trying to get around me, Mr. Blake, so I won't feel badly about your being hired."

Vic grinned, laughed, and Dale was sure he was about to lean over the counter and kiss Mrs. Inness' cheek. "You're right, and you're wrong, Mrs. Inness. I am conning you, but I am also promising. Those little brats, in case Dale hasn't told you already, are deeply involved with the loss of my job. Believe me, they'll toe the mark while they're in here."

"And if they—"

A sudden screeching of metal, shattering of glass, stunned them into silence. An explosion and a quickening of the light.

"Oh God, now what?" Vic said, opening the door and moving out to the sidewalk. He looked down the street, turned back and beckoned quickly. Dale couldn't hear what he was saying, but the name he called out was clear enough.

"David Campbell?" Bella said, her voice breaking in shock.

Once outside, Dale saw Campbell's automobile canted up a telephone pole. It was blanketed in flames, while smoldering pieces had smashed through nearby shop windows. A crowd was trying to get closer, several men with their arms over their faces attempting to snatch open the driver's door. Beyond the pole was something lying on the macadam. As Dale ran up, tears already breaking, she saw that it was what was left of Willy's father; apparently forced through the windshield, sliced by the glass, only his head, arms and torso had been thrown clear of the wreck. She gagged and spun around as the men trying to get into the car realized what had happened and one dropped a coat over the remains.

It was too much, now. She felt as if she were carrying a curse with her. A scolding, still rational part of her mind told her it was coincidence and she'd better not start looking for superstitious nonsense; but she couldn't help feeling that somehow she was going to be part of this tragedy, too.

Bella had stayed by the shop and took Dale's arms, guided her inside. "My poor dear," she muttered, "you look like . . ."

"Thanks," Dale said, knowing the word the woman had avoided. "Have . . . have you got anything in the back? Something brewing, or a little stronger?"

"I have just the thing," the woman said and left her at the counter to hurry into the back office.

Dale leaned heavily against the door jamb, her stomach roiling. She shook her head and thought of Milly and Flora, wondering how they would manage now that their paycheck was gone. Cold you are, she thought, and in searching for something to distract her, she spotted an odd piece of paper covering the receipt Bella had written earlier. She stared at it, seeing the childish scrawl but not able to read it.

Her hand trembled when it reached out, and yanked the paper off the nail.

"What is it?" Bella said, coming up behind her with a drinking glass filled with brandy.

"Another love note," Dale said.

She closed her eyes when Bella took it from her. Saw the mutilated corpse, an object by its bloodied hand. It was small, possibly wrenched from an angered, clenched fist.

"I don't understand," Bella said.

Dale waved the paper away. She didn't want to touch it.

*Miss Bartlett*, it said, *we missed you at the park*.

# CHAPTER
# IV

"For crying out loud, that was two months ago!"

They were walking along Chancellor Avenue back toward the center of town with the park at their right. It had been Dale's idea, to escape the commotion of the accident and the smothering consolations Mrs. Inness felt the situation warranted. Vic had protested as they passed Dale's house, suggesting they stop for a drink instead. But she'd refused, not knowing why, only partially admitting she would have felt uncomfortable with a man in the place, alone. Onward, then, until he demanded they turn around. And when they did, her mood had soured instead of lightened.

"And this definitely couldn't have been from him," she added, waving the paper in front of his face.

"No kidding, Dale. That much is obvious from the use of the word 'we' instead of 'I.' "

"All right, then, wise guy—who is 'we'?"

Vic shrugged, picked up a stick from the ground and rattled it along the iron fencing. When she asked him to stop it, he broke the stick into pieces and flung them up and into the trees. "All right, then, the kids. They must have known about that first note and are playing a game. Okay?"

"Oh sure." She tugged at her hair, then shoved a finger angrily through it. "That's not going to work, Vic. I mean, how long can the attention span of a kid be, huh? Do you really think they'd pick on that love-note nonsense now? After all this time? No way, teacher, no way."

"Fine, have it your way. So it wasn't the kids. Maybe it has no connection at all. I don't know, lady, I'm just guessing. You're the one who's making a big deal out of it."

They were opposite the house again and Dale, furious at Vic's inability to solve her problem, stopped and moved to the curb. "This," she said stiffly, "is where I get off."

"For God's sake, Dale, come off it!"

"If you don't mind, I think I'd like to be alone. Or isn't that all right with you?"

He frowned, seemed ready to explode, then blew out a deep breath and stared at the sky. "No, that's fine with me. You just trot on home." He glanced at his watch. "I'll just wander on down to the Inn and grab something to eat before my landlady makes me have some of her godawful Irish stew."

"Is that a thinly veiled invitation?"

"No."

She glared, turned, and strode across the street, up the walk to the porch where she stood with her back to the road for several long seconds before looking back over her shoulder. She muttered a curse when she saw Vic already crossing the Park Street corner.

There was a fleeting hesitation, and an impulse to run after him; but she only dropped to the top step and cupped her hands to her chin. It had been a stupid argument. She had expected too much. When she had finally described her nightmare to him, and he'd suggested the first note had been from Willy, her subconscious suspected as much and was still dredging up a spanking in an effort to convince her she might have saved the boy's life had she found the note sooner and gone to the park to meet him.

A car sped by, horn blaring loudly, several boys within calling to her as they passed. Now there's the more likely answer, she thought as she watched the car out of sight. High school boys with a crush. They probably knew she spent a great deal of time, particularly her lunch hours, in the park; they had spied on her as an ideal opportunity to get a good look at the woman they thought they were in love with.

She smiled and shook her head.

Boys. They weren't all that much different from men in that respect—shy and aggressive, brimming with a protective shield of brashness that, once punctured, revealed a core of masculine insecurity.

Boys. Men. Victor Blake.

Flora and Milly Campbell. Whatever her own problems, they were as nothing to the distaff Campbells. What a horrid thing to happen, and so soon after the boy, too. God, she thought, there sure is a perversity to life that sometimes makes you want to scream.

It was like a twist on a saying that one of her

professors was fond of quoting: *If all the world's a stage and all the people merely players, who's the jerk who hired the Director?*

She went inside and fixed herself a meal too bland to taste, too weak to keep her satisfied for more than two hours. At nine, then, she decided to walk down to the luncheonette and get herself the largest ice cream sundae she could find on the menu; that, she thought, ought to keep her pacified until breakfast.

A digital clock in a jewelry-store window indicated close to ten-thirty by the time she had finished her sundae, joked with the night counterman, and left. Her legs were heavy, her arms two lead pipes, and she couldn't see herself doing this on a Sunday and getting up in the morning to open the store. As she turned the corner onto Chancellor, she looked at the houses slowly displacing the two-story business-district buildings. An old twinge of envy for their owners made her lower her head and stare at the sidewalk. It must be nice, she thought, to be able to work a five-day week, to get home every night for supper and not have to go back to work again. The vacation had spoiled her, had given her something she hadn't known she was missing until she came face to face with it. Of course it was possible Vic might help to alter that—if he caught on rapidly enough and was good enough, she might be able to trade off Saturdays with him and Bella. One on and two off, or some such arrangement. A two-day weekend just like normal people.

She paused at the corner of the park and leaned against one iron spindle of the fence. One block to home. One very long block. She yawned and considered sleeping where she stood. The day's heat had cooled, more so because of the light mist that settled soothing droplets on her face and bare arms. The street lights had a faint haze about them, and she frowned when she saw the two nearest her house had blown out again. High school kids and airguns, the police thought; but they had never been caught at it, and so it continued throughout the village until, in some places, globes weren't replaced for days at a time. In the long run it probably saved time, she thought, not that Oxrun needed to save money—but it made for a dismal walk home.

She pushed off the fence and walked, her fingers gliding along the metal as Vic had done with his stick. There were no cars and Chancellor Avenue seemed a long diminishing tunnel that led nowhere, from nowhere, and the cracking slap of her sandals was unduly loud.

When she came opposite Western she stepped over the grass verge to the curb and looked down the street that ran past the house. She tried to remember what was down there, how far it went before it was cut off by the forest that poked its extensions into Oxrun wherever houses had encroached. She tried to remember, and couldn't, and had just about made up her mind to take a walk in that direction when something turned her around.

Imagination, she decided. Beyond the fence was the black void that became a park when the sun rose. What she thought she heard was a rustling in the brush, decided almost instantly it was either nightbirds or stray cats prowling for a meal.

She heard it again.

Softer. Further down the road. It wasn't a rustling. It was a whispering, a conversation between more than two people. She lifted her gold wristwatch close to her face. Nearly eleven. The park gates had been long closed and locked, and the lovers who defied the curfew generally chose places deeper into the trees.

She glanced back toward the center of town. A dairy's delivery truck momentarily blinded her before turning off, its faint rumble almost like a receding clap of thunder. A patrol car glided slowly away from her. When it too turned into a side street, Chancellor was deserted.

It has to be lovers, she thought, and this is no time to be playing at voyeur.

A shout, then, cut off by a flurry of whispers.

Dale cautiously moved back to the sidewalk, bending and slipping her sandals into her hands. She was cold damp and, in spite of the muggy night, glad she hadn't worn shorts. She crept forward slowly, once glancing over her shoulder at her house as it passed her and wishing she'd left the porch light on. Then she stepped off the walk onto the narrow band of grass and weeds that had escaped under the fence. By straining she could just make out the vague shapes of trees and shrubs, but without the moon there was little else. She frowned, wiping a hand against her leg. If the light on the street was so terribly bad, she couldn't understand why those inside didn't even have a match—and suddenly she knew they didn't because its glow would have been visible for at least a full block. She had a disconcerting vision, then: of small twisted creatures covered with slime and fur, their saucer eyes wide to pick up the faintest illumination. It made her shiver, and she scolded herself out of the first stirrings of apprehension felt since she decided to eavesdrop.

A moment later she dropped into an uncomfortable crouch. Whoever was making the noise was less than ten feet ahead of her now, and she didn't dare move closer lest she be seen. Yet it was dark where she was; not even a light from the houses opposite broke through the mist that had thickened to a gray, clammy fog. She took a small step forward. A sandal clattered against the fence and she froze, holding her breath, staring unblinking at a lonely dandelion quivering in a breeze she couldn't feel. The fog shortened the street, curtained off everything more than a yard away.

The whispering resumed.

Her breathing returned.

A thundering began in the depths of the fog.

She swore silently.

The thundering grew. The fog became lighter in two uneven patches. A cat ran across the road; the strident blare of an air horn shattered the night as an oil truck barreled past and its headlights, yellow running lights, diesel engine trampled, dispersed, blew away the fog.

And when it was gone, there was the fog and the street.

Nothing else.

Dale waited impatiently, edging nearer to the point of the whispering; but whoever it had been was gone. She sensed it but remained in her crouch until her thighs began to ache the threat of a cramp. Finally, she grabbed the fence and pulled herself up. She dropped her sandals and slipped her feet into them, kicking at the grass before turning to stare boldly into the park. There was no need for caution now—she was alone.

And that, she thought as she headed back to the house, is the perfect way to end a rotten day.

Like an insect that couldn't be found when the lights were turned on, the whispering stayed with her. She showered and kept the water drumming loudly in the stall, but the whispering stayed with her. She sang as she undressed and walked heel hard into the bedroom—but the whispering stayed with her.

And when she closed her eyes, the nightstand light glowing softly, the whispering grew louder until she shouted it from the room in a rush of obscenities that startled her into silence when she realized what she'd been saying.

''All right, then,'' she said, and turned off the light.

The window was open, the shade up and curtains drawn back. A single rectangle of faint white. She stared at the ceiling, waiting for sleep, and remembered the last time she had spoken with Dave Campbell. It had only been the week before; he had come into the store with a set of chessmen carvings—oddly designed, resembling primitive stone statuettes aged a centuries-old gray. Yet when she hefted one, she'd nearly dropped it in surprise at its light weight.

David, his laugh as deep as his frame was large,

had taken it carefully from her palm and replaced it in the oblong black box he'd made to carry the set.

"My God, Dave," she said, "it must have taken you years to finish these off."

"Long enough," he agreed, then put his hands behind his back and rocked on his heels.

"Ah," she smiled, "the haggling begins." She set the case in front of her and eyed the cotton-packed carvings. "Now, if we were in the city, there'd be no problem at all getting at least one hundred fifty for men and board."

"But we're not in the city, Dale," he said.

"True. Oxrun Station is definitely not the city. It is, in fact, a million miles into the country. However" —and she raised a finger—"what we have here in the Station is something you don't find in such abundance in that mean old city."

"Money," Dave laughed.

"Money," she said. "So if I can't get at least three hundred for such exquisite work, I'm no businesswoman."

Dave's eyes had widened and his hands snapped back front in a pleading gesture. "Three hundred? But that's too much. Nobody will—"

"David Campbell, why don't you just leave the gathering of the loot to me? After all, wasn't it me who got you three fifty for those silkie pieces, and you thought we should ask only ninety-five? Wasn't it my brilliant fast thinking and talking that pried five fifty from Councilman Hopkins for the mahogany pipe band set? And wasn't—"

"You win, you win!" he laughed. "Three hundred it is. Unless you hit Hopkins again, in which case you can aim a little higher."

She grinned and reached over the counter to jab at his shoulder. "You're learning, David Campbell. You're learning."

"Not nearly fast enough," he muttered, smiling weakly and turning to leave. Dale immediately whistled him to a halt.

"If you don't mind," she said, "would you tell me what they're supposed to be in case someone asks?"

"Oh." He touched the figures gently, as if in silent benediction. "They are of the myths," he said, and there was an echo of his aunt's Highland burr. "The darker ones are the Children of Don, the lighter be the Children of Llyr." And as he named them . . . "Govannan, Ludd, Gwydion" . . . the store grew quiet . . . "Arianrod, Llew, Bendegeit, Bran" . . . the light through the window became a glare and she was forced to squint, lean closer to follow his heavily pointing finger . . . "Manawyddan, the rooks be the fortress Gower, the pawns here the Hound of Culann, and here they are the water-dog—what we call the otter."

And when he looked up into her eyes, she saw the tears brimming, his thin, pale lips drawn in between his teeth.

"Sell them well," he said quietly. "A traveler would be best."

She rolled over onto her stomach and punched at the pillow. The scene faded as quickly as it had been conjured, but she was positive he'd added something else before hurrying from the store. She made a fist and tapped her forehead lightly, then more strongly. It had only been a passing utterance, a few words hung in the store's cool air and vanishing as the door closed and she'd watched him lumbering up the street.

Come on, she told herself, you of the fantastic memory ought to be able to remember a few short words.

*I wish I knew, fire or water.*

All right, she said silently; now that you've got them what are you going to do with them?

Remember them, she answered; for Dave.

The set had been displayed less than two days before Dr. McPherson had passed by, seen it, and bowled over three small girls waiting at the counter in his eagerness to have it. Bella had taken the money, for which Dale was extremely sorry—if such covetousness could pry that kind of payment so easily, she might have been able to add an extra hundred or two. And then there was Dave's unusual request to sell it to a traveler. An out-of-towner, she thought he meant.

Not that it mattered now.

David was no longer in a position to spend anything she would have gotten beyond their original agreement.

And the following night her nightmares returned.

The water, the sinking, the bubbles, the stench. Each time she sank more swiftly, and each time the face in the cloud became clearer, more malevolent. Again three days later, and three days after that. By the end of the second week she was afraid of taking a nap. And it was less the coming of the dream itself than the not knowing when it would appear again. She tried to find a key, something during the preceding days that might have triggered each shuddering premonition of her death; but there was nothing that she could see, nothing she might have avoided. Vic was doing well, sufficiently so that she was able to inaugurate the alternate Saturday plan with no qualms. No, it wasn't Vic, and Bella's inexplicable attacks of continuing good cheer were hardly a catalyst for such terror.

Neither rhyme nor reason, then, were cause for such fright.

The dream changed. A hint of a change. A hint of a flame on the rim of the cloud.

**It** changed.

On the last day of September Dale sat in front of the library. There were four benches on the perimeter of a large square of deep green grass, an island in the middle of a concrete plaza. Opposite her, two elderly men played checkers on a board precariously balanced across their knees. Every so often they glanced up and smiled at her, and when she smiled back they returned to their game, nodding. Williamston Pike was crowded with traffic, people scurrying out of the Station as if they sensed this would be the last decent weekend before October's autumn chills set in and spoiled the twilights that were still cozily comfortable. The sun set nearer to six each day, lost more of its brilliance sooner, poked back to the world a few minutes earlier. The building-tall gray glass windows behind her hid the hanging lamps inside, but she knew it would not open until at least nine.

Plenty of time, she thought, to get up enough nerve to go inside and search out a book that might help explain her dreams. Maybe Nat Clayton . . . but Dale didn't want to reveal too much, and in deciding that realized that for a woman her age she had no real female friends in whom she could confide. It had always been her mother, and since taking over the store she had convinced herself she was far too busy to cultivate the frivolous.

Now she regretted it, half hoped Natalie would come striding out on her way to meet her husband, the editor of the local newspaper. There was no serious thought of speaking to Bella; the old woman, she knew, would only homily her to death and pass it off as a phase all young women endured while waiting for a husband.

The players. She watched them set up a new game. With age comes wisdom, she thought for no reason at all; maybe they could help me since they don't even know who I am. And as the temptation to interrupt them grew stronger, she tried not to smile, to grin, to break into laughter. She was ready to leave, then, before she succumbed when a shadow darkened the concrete at her feet. Startled, she looked up and back, and relaxed.

"Ed," she said in mock scolding, "it isn't polite for local shrinks to sneak up on unescorted ladies like that."

McPherson tugged at his forelock in apology and moved to sit beside her, maintaining a carefully wide space between them. "You looked rather lonely, Dale, and I decided to see what was bothering you. Troubles at the store?"

The long face, the heavy brows that glowered over his eyes were set in such an obvious attitude of professional attention that she couldn't help but laugh aloud, more so when he frowned puzzlement and began rubbing the side of his nose vigorously. The old men, she saw, hurriedly swept their pieces into coat pockets and scurried off to the library without a glance in her direction. McPherson ignored them or, she thought, more likely hadn't even known they were there.

"Ed," she said, sobering, "I'm sorry, but you look so . . . so officebound sitting there. Don't you ever relax?"

He glanced sheepishly at his crossed legs, his hands placed just so in his lap. He tried to assume a more casual position, with one arm draped along the back of the bench.

"A habit," he said. "People seem to expect it of me so I naturally comply before I even read the signs." He pulled a cigarette from a crushed pack in his jacket pocket. She declined his offer of one, watched as he lighted it and shoved the burnt match into a pocket. "So. I'm relaxed."

"Good for you," she said.

"So tell me anyway. What's with the long face? Man trouble?"

"Oh, brother, don't I wish. No, I've got sleep troubles."

"The store, right?"

"You know something, Doc," she said, pushing herself into a corner so she could see him without turning her head, "for a man who makes a living unbending folks' minds, you sure don't know how to fish very well. Why don't you just say: Dale, do you want to tell me what's bothering you?"

"All right," he said, smiling. "Dale, do you want to tell me what's bothering you?"

"No, not really," she said, laughing anew when his lips opened in surprise and the cigarette fell to the ground. But as he scrambled for it and straightened, she decided there was no reason why she shouldn't get an expert's opinion instead of rooting through musty library shelves with no real idea of what she was seeking, no notion of what it would be when she found it. "Dreams," she said finally, softly. "Well, not dreams exactly. One dream is more the case. I had it once a month or so ago, more than that I think, and several times over the past few weeks." She described it to him, hugging herself as the cloud superimposed itself in the air over the Pike. And when she'd done, she looked at him and was disappointed. He only sat there, staring, with no hint of revelation, no beaming grin. Just a stare that passed through her as if she wasn't there.

She smiled; the smile faded.

"Well?" she prodded. "How crazy am I?"

"No crazier than anyone else, Dale. That much I can tell you without a fee."

"Oh come on! You mean you're going to charge me for this outdoor session?"

"I was kidding, Dale."

She shrugged. Ed's one major fault—one among many, she corrected herself—was his inability to signal to others that he was trying, though failing, to be humorous. "I thought maybe it was guilt or something about Willy Campbell's death. You know . . . not being able to save him and all."

"Well, you thought rightly, Dale. That's exactly

what it seems to be. It's one thing to tell yourself in the mirror, to intellectualize if you will, that it is precisely what you said . . . but it's quite another to let your subconscious guilt feelings in on the dialogue. The . . . what shall we say? . . . the hatred the boy's face appears to project your way isn't his reproach for your seeming—and I stress that word 'seeming'— failure to save him. It's your own interpretation of how he might feel if he were in any shape to feel anything at all. It was, simply and unalterably, a freak accident which you were powerless to avert and unable to thwart the consequences of. Since you had seen him only a couple of hours earlier, it's only natural that your shock at finding him drowned be all the greater. And when the second death occurred, that of his father which was also something you weren't able to prevent, all you did was equate the two in your mind and what you get . . . is a beaut of a nightmare.''

She listened carefully, following without much difficulty as he continued, repeating himself several times though the message was the same. And it was true. So simply true that it was small wonder she couldn't convince herself of it. What it took was the word of a professional.

''You see,'' he concluded, his hands spread wide, ''complexity is not always involved in something like this. By taking my word for it, and thereby seeing yourself how right I am, you shouldn't be bothered again. Maybe once more for good measure, but beyond that, well . . .'' and he slapped his leg, making her jump.

Her smile was weak, and a helpless feeling of the

ridiculous made her refuse to meet his gaze. Finally she held out her hand and he took it. His palm was warm, dry, and she pulled her hand away as if she were a schoolgirl again, meeting the football god she'd admired only from the sidelines.

"Well," he said after an awkwardly long silence, "so how's business?"

She blinked, put a hand to her cheek, and rubbed slowly. "Well enough, thanks. Which reminds me—how are you enjoying that chess set you bought? I should warn you that if I'd been there instead of Mrs. Inness, I probably would have tried to goose up the price a bit."

Ed laughed dutifully. "And well you could have, Dale. It is without a doubt the prize of my meager collection. So much so, in fact, that I never use it for games. It just sits on my mantel where I can stare at it."

"An expensive stare, if you ask me," she said.

He took a deep breath, lighted another cigarette. "With only a son to watch over, I can afford such things. And besides, it's far too rare to fool around with."

"One of a kind," she said quietly, thinking of Dave and the way he had called off their names.

"Indeed it is," Ed said briskly, and rose suddenly. "But that's the way life is, you know, as much as one tends to hate it for being that way. And now that you've brought it up, I think I'll go home and have a good, long, expensive stare at old Gower and company again. Something to ease my mind after a hard day's work at the bench."

She didn't stand but rather twisted around on the

bench. "Hey, Ed!" she called as he headed down the Pike. "Did you say Gower and company?"

McPherson stopped, not turning until several seconds had passed. "Why, yes, I did. The rooks, you know. Gower Castle."

"How'd you know that?"

He put a hand to his chin, then shrugged. "To tell you the truth, I don't really know. Dave must have told me, I guess. Or a bit of esoterica that pops up in my fertile and useless mind once in a while."

"Oh. Okay," she said.

"Why?"

She shook her head. "No reason. I just remembered what Dave told me about them, and I didn't think anyone else knew what they were supposed to be. And why I thought that I just don't know."

He smiled. "You're only annoyed because it was just another selling point to help part me from my money."

"Hey, I'm not annoyed, Ed. I just didn't expect you to . . ." She waved the words away. "Forget it. It's not important. Esoterica, as you said."

"Right. Now I really must go, Dale. Take care of yourself, will you? And should those dreams come back, don't be too shy about calling me, okay? You know where you can find me."

He waved, walked briskly away while Dale resettled herself to face the traffic and wonder why his knowing about the Children of Don, the Children of Llyr should bother her.

"It shouldn't, and it doesn't," she told herself firmly. "And if you believe that, Dale Bartlett, I'll tell you another."

# CHAPTER
# V

The night was still, the air like a sheath of thin ice over black water. The sky was filled with staring stars, the roads crisscrossed with shadows from moon and street lamps.

Dale stood on the broad open porch of a blue Victorian home still gleaming with a summer coat of paint. Diagonally opposite was the sedate amber glow of the Chancellor Inn, the half-lit parking lot where Vic had left his car. As he rang the doorbell he looked down at her with an apologetic grin. She smiled encouragement while thinking the evening shouldn't be all that bad, even if her hostess would be Liz Provence. A few hours away from the house had been Vic's persuasive argument, a chance for her to loosen up and get drunk if she wanted to, at least have an opportunity to reacquaint herself with the rest of the world.

Privately, she'd also decided it would be a night of celebration. For over three weeks since her library session with Ed McPherson, her sleep had been undisturbed by the face in the cloud. Though she had afterward questioned his quick, seemingly superficial diagnosis, something there must have reached her subconscious because it and the water were gone. So . . . a chance to laugh, to lift a glass or three, and get home at whatever hour she chose because the following day was Sunday and the wrong side of noon was reserved for those who needed the sunrise to wake up to.

Within the house were explosions of laughter, the faint and unintelligible shouts of men already halfway through the famous Provence punchbowl. There was music, but all she felt was a thudding bass that threatened to shake down the walls. While not necessarily the socially imperative place to be seen, Liz's parties had always held a snakelike fascination for her, a last resort for the not-quite-rich of the Station to mend their wounds for not being invited to the affairs in the estates on the other side of the park.

"Maybe," she said finally, "she knows it's us and won't let us in."

"Not funny," Vic grumbled, blowing into his hands and stamping his feet. "It's that stereo of hers. I think she's trying to turn the place into a rocketship or something." He pressed the bell again, held it until he snorted in exasperation and opened the door. "In!" he shouted over the noise that flooded onto the porch. "We'll announce ourselves and wait to be thrown out."

The tiny foyer, already jammed with benches and

chairs hidden under topcoats, was separated from the
house by a paned-glass door through which Dale
could see the drifting, swirling party. Women in light
gowns and billowing slacks, see-through blouses and
rainbow caftans; men in suits, leisure jackets, printed
shirts and jeans. Vic took her coat and his and jammed
them into an overflowing closet. He wore a black
corduroy jacket and open-necked shirt, Dale a glint-
ing green satin blouse and matching skirt. After a
quick mutual appraisal, flicking imaginary lint off
shoulders and elbows, they opened the second door,
and flinched.

The music deafened, the conversations shouted,
and just below the ceiling writhed a blue-gray pall of
smoke that resisted the efforts of open windows to
disperse it. Indecision froze them momentarily, then
Vic took her arm and led her to the right through an
arch into a large dining room in which a buffet had
been spread on a massive circular table. Glasses
empty and glasses half-filled littered the window sills
and the spaces on the tablecloth where heaping plates
of sandwiches had been picked over. Streamers hung
limply from a crystal chandelier and deflated bal-
loons shifted weakly as people passed uncaringly
beneath them. Vic sighed loudly, grabbed two plates
and filled them while Dale snatched a glass of champagne from a passing waiter and drank it without
stopping.

She was bored already, and already began a fight
to keep Vic from noticing.

Most of the food was tepid. Some of it soggy.
Dale grimaced, forced herself to eat not because she

was hungry but because she wanted as large a foun-
dation in her stomach for her drinking as she could
get. It was going to be that kind of a night, she
thought. A long, long one.

Vic evidently felt the same way. He gulped down
one sandwich, winced, and returned the plate to the
table. Then he pulled her into a corner and searched
the room for someone they knew. Failing that, he
groaned and leaned down to be heard.

"I don't see Liz anywhere," he said.

"If we're lucky, she'll be lost for the rest of the
night. How did you get invited to one of these things?"

"Pure chance," he laughed. "She wants my su-
perb form to grace her bed for an evening."

Dale punched him, harder than she thought, and
quickly rubbed his chest. A woman in red stopped
and stared through glazed eyes, swayed toward them
and swerved abruptly away. Dale stuck out her tongue
at the backless dress and Vic yanked on her hair.

"How many times have I told you, you have the
wrong attitude about life?" he said.

"This is life? Ye gods, pray for the angel Gabriel."

He chuckled, grabbed two glasses from a tray carried by a harried-looking man in a rumpled waiter's
uniform. The man stopped, glared, swept himself
away into an adjoining room. Dale stuck her tongue
out again, then yelped when Vic clipped her lightly
under the chin, forcing her teeth to bite down.

"Hey, that hurt!"

"You think that's bad, just wait a minute," he
said, nodding toward the room on the other side of
the foyer.

Dale poked her head around the jamb and sighed. Liz Provence was coming toward them, her face gleaming with perspiration, her thick lips working as she whispered to a bald-headed man beside her. Dale knew she was close to forty and did her best to hide it: her black hair was brushed to a sheen and lay delicately on rounded bare shoulders, her face handsome in the Roman manner. Her figure she displayed in a simple black cocktail dress that barely reached the center of her thighs, flowed out from her hips to give the illusion of motion even as she remained still. The neckline was high, and between her breasts dangled a gold chain without pendant.

They tried to duck back into their corner, but Liz had spotted them. She dismissed her escort with an imperial wave and turned to confront them, smiling, her hand out for Vic to take and bow slightly over, for Dale to touch and release without even feeling the contact.

"Vic, Dale," she said with a *moue* and a shake of her hair, "it's about time someone with a little wit and intelligence showed up. I don't know why I bother with these things. It's so damned masochistic."

"Nonsense," Vic said politely. "It looks like everyone is having a fine time."

"Yes," Dale said, standing decidedly closer to him. "If noise is any indication, these folks aren't going to forget this one for a long time."

Liz lowered her high, thin eyebrows slightly, turned away for a moment when the waiter returned to whisper something in her ear. Dale looked to Vic for a conspiratorial exchange, but he was preoccupied with Liz's figure. She wanted to punch him then, hard. But a voice called her name, and she waved too heartily at one of the store's regulars. The faces came into sharp focus immediately thereafter and she recognized more of the merchants who shared her block, the bankers and jewelers whose establishments took up almost the entire opposite side of the street. They saw her, nodded or smiled or beckoned out of courtesy, and she returned the gestures with broad demurrals of her own. Sooner or later she knew she would be caught up with them, exchanging gossip, sniping at Liz behind her back—but at the moment she decided it wouldn't hurt to let Liz know that she had a stake in the ex-teacher and wasn't about to release it without a skirmish.

"Crap." Liz's exclamation snapped Dale back to the party, made her blink as she watched the hostess bend over and take off her shoes to hold in one hand while she rubbed her soles without leaning against either of them for balance. "You know, Dale, these things are a drag. If that slimy waiter tries once more to get me upstairs, I'm going to shove his tray where it'll do the most good. And I doubt that he'll take the hint."

Dale laughed in spite of herself, was about to comment, when a second waiter, far broader than any man had a right to be, interrupted and pleaded with Liz to allow him to open another case of champagne. Liz tightened her lips, tapped one bare foot angrily before nodding sharply.

"And that one," she said glumly, "is the worst organizer in the whole universe. Brother, am I tired!"

Suddenly the mask slipped, the face shouted its

weariness and well-disguised disgust at what Liz was doing. Dale couldn't resist a hand to her shoulder and was surprised when Liz covered it briefly before turning and Dale had to pull back. And it was a reluctant move because Dale had seen something in the Provence woman she'd never expected was there: a humanness that instantly brought her down from her artificial Olympus and reinstated her with the rest of the normal living. It was a revelation she wanted to share, but Vic had gone, vanished into the crowd.

"You know," Liz said, "when you put the ring in the nose, it's always best to leave a few yards of rope slack. Otherwise they think it's only jewelry."

"What?" Dale turned back into a broad grin. "I'm sorry, Liz, I was . . ." And she was confused, the heat of the corner bringing perspiration to her upper lip. She dabbed at it with her sleeve, emptied another glass and set it on the window sill behind her.

"Relax, Dale, will you?"

She grinned. "Funny, but people keep telling me that. I must look like a zombie."

"Not quite. Stand near the waiter with the bald spot and you'll find out how you look."

A surge of guests from the back room inadvertently pushed Liz closer. Dale shrank away, felt the wall at her back and stiffened. She didn't like the closeness. It was too much like being locked into a glass-walled closet. Quickly she cleared her throat.

"Liz, I'm sorry, but Vic never told me—is this party in honor of something or other?"

"Of course, but I forget what it is." She lifted a wrist to stare at a watch hidden among a display of

diamonds. "But whatever it is, it's now time for the
hunt. The highlight of this gala farce." She touched
Dale's arm, smiled and hurried away to the living
room, guests at her back, the music suddenly stopping in midchord. Dale followed, and cursed when
she saw she would have to stand in the foyer. Pushing up on her toes, she saw Liz on an upholstered
bench in front of a blackfaced fireplace. She only
heard half of what was said, but understood enough
to know that the so-called highlight would be an
old-fashioned scavenger hunt, the prize for which
was a pewter mug Liz displayed with a flourish.

Oh, for God's sake, Dale thought. Who wants to
play such a childish . . . and she stopped herself. If
Vic was determined that she break out of the shell
her dream had built around her, and if she was going
to salvage a good time, why not be part of a scavenger hunt? Why should all the fun in the world be
reserved for kids? A tug at her sleeve interrupted her
thoughts, and Vic was at her side, a piece of green
mimeo paper in one hand.

"Come on," he said, pulling her. She resisted and
he glared at the ceiling, shook the paper under her
nose and pulled again. "Will you come on, lady?
I've got our list here, and if we don't get going,
we're not going to win."

A battle for their coats, a race for the car, and they
were speeding toward the toy store. Part of the list
included tools and children's clothes, and Dale vol-
unteered the thought that since size wasn't mentioned, dolls' clothes would do as well. Vic had

kissed her. She beamed, and when the car pulled to the curb, they were in and out in less than five minutes. Laughing. Shouting. Not caring what the rest of the world thought as they constructed their fun.

Vic pulled away from the store before Dale had a chance to shut her door.

"Hey," she said, trying to catch her breath from laughing so loudly, "we're not the Capone mob, you know."

"More's the pity," he said. "What's next?"

She held the paper close to her face, trying to sort out what they had found from what they needed.

"Remember," he said, "we can't use our houses."

"I have many dirty thoughts about that," she said. "Now. We need yellow chalk and an apple. That's it."

"Great," he said, applying the brakes and skidding into a U-turn. "We'll save the apple for last. I know where we can get the chalk."

"Hey, Vic," she said, sobering slightly. "You're not going to break into the school, are you?"

"And who has a better right," he grunted as he took a corner too tightly and bounced over the curb.

She would have protested, but when she saw the expression of devilish delight made fiendish by the dashboard's glow, she resigned herself and glanced at the rear view mirror, half expecting Fred Borg's patrol car to be flashing its blue-and-red at them. There was a car, she noticed with a guilty start, but when Vic pulled into the small parking lot behind the high school building, it continued on without slow-ing. They drove, then, to the building's far corner, beyond the reach of street lights and passing cars.

"Now," he said, braking, "you stay here. I'll be back in a flash."

"Sure," she said, sliding behind the wheel as he left. "And don't break anything, will you? I'm going to have a hard enough time explaining the store's mess to Bella on Monday; I don't want to have to say a thing to the police."

"Don't be a spoilsport. Honk twice if there's trouble." And he was gone, heading for a basement window hidden behind three large garbage collection dumpsters. The car creaked as engine heat escaped, and in the distance she heard a siren trailing. A leaf scrabbled across the hood, and she pounded on the steering wheel excitedly, as though the gesture would make Vic move faster. With the window down she was getting cold, but she didn't want to turn on the blower to pull in residual warmth in case she needed to hear something. Instead she blew on her palms and rubbed her cheeks. A car passed, and she ducked onto the seat until its lights swept over and beyond her. The siren died.

"Come on, come on, come on!" she whispered. Leaning out the window, she looked up at the school. There was nothing, no betrayal of Vic's presence inside. Suppose the night watchman discovered him, she thought. Suppose he'd heard Vic coming in and the police were already there waiting to spring a trap. A minute, and she worried that he had taken a fall down the steel-edged steps, or stumbled over a chair and struck his head on a desk. She stared, squinting, and thought she spotted a shade rippling on the third floor. Sitting back, then, she sighed heavily, and the windshield fogged in front of her. It was ridiculous, two grown people sneaking around a place like Oxrun Station after chalk and apples and God knows what else. Whatever had made her think this would be fun? It certainly wasn't amusing waiting for the police to ride up beside her and demand to know what she was doing sitting in a darkened parking lot in the middle of the night with a pile of tools and toys in the back seat.

"Well, Officer, it's like this, see," and she laughed at the sound of her voice, wiped a hand over her face, and was ready to slip out to follow him when Vic suddenly appeared in front of the car, a small box clutched in his hand. Immediately she moved over to give him room, grabbed his arm when he was in and kissed him on the cheek.

"For that," he said, "I'd climb the building naked."

"Later," she said, bouncing on the seat. "Did you get it?"

He held out the box. "Dozens of pieces, all colors. Alice Franklin never leaves her room locked at night. Some kind of phobia. I didn't have time to check, but there has to be at least one piece of yellow in there."

"Fine," she said, tossing it into the back. "Now where are we going to get an apple?"

"No stores?"

"This late on a Saturday? We're not in the big bad city, you know, fella."

"All right, then," he said, pulling out to the street, "there's only one place left."

• • •

Vic parked a few yards in from the corner of High and the Mainland Road. Directly opposite was a series of fields decades untended, slowly reclaimed by relentless incursions of evergreen and oak. A straggling thorned hedge separated the fields from the highway, and with no facing homes, Oxrun was effectively hidden from the light passing traffic.

"Now wait a minute," Dale protested. "If you think I'm going to traipse across those fields to old man Armstrong's orchard just to get one lousy fresh apple—"

But Vic was already out and around, opening her door and tugging on her sleeve. She resisted, relented, and stood with him on the corner waiting for a chance to cross.

"Dumb," she muttered.

"But fun, lady. Come on and admit it, Dale! You haven't let loose like this in years, and you know it."

She looked at him carefully; and when he smiled, leaned over and kissed her cheek, touched a fingertip to her nose, she shivered and decided he wasn't so terribly bad after all, and neither was the game they were playing.

"Now!" he ordered suddenly and ran across the highway, slid down the ditch, and was halfway up the other side before Dale could catch up. A few minutes' fumbling and they darted through a narrow gap in the hedge.

The field was broad, weeds knee- and waist-high that hid the furrows not yet pounded smooth by the years that had passed since they were last used. Solitary trees were ragged patches against the black, grasping it seemed for the stars just out of reach. Dale turned around and looked over the hedge to the village.

Vic took her shoulder, followed her gaze. "To think," he said, "that such a beautiful place is now filled with screaming maniacs like us, playing at hunting for treasure."

"Nice," she said, and allowed herself to be kissed while her hands stroked his arms. Then, with a shake and a playful slap to his head, she broke away. "March," she ordered. "Let's get this nonsense over with. I know just where I can put that pewter thing."

"Now wait just a minute," he said, following. "What about me? What do I get out of all this?"

"If you're a good boy," she called over her shoulder, "a nice cup of hot chocolate in the sanctity of my kitchen."

"Well, then," he said, and ran after her, laughing, then tripped and sprawled with a shower of curses into the dead weeds and grass.

It was impossible to move rapidly. Despite moonglow and stars, and the faint illumination of widely spaced highway lights, there were too many ground shadows camouflaging burrows and hollows that trapped their shoes and wrenched at their ankles. The orchard, some two hundred yards ahead, once belonging to the Armstrong family, was now wild and untended and had been that way since Dale and her parents had come here with the fresh bite of autumn to pick the fruit that remained. But the trees died one by one as vines strangled and seasons stared, and though new trees sometimes survived, the orchard had shrunk from its original hundreds to a lonely handful that seldom carried its apples to term. Dale thought of this as she stumbled over the rough ground. It was dry, and the fallen weeds broke like twigs beneath her, and the earth was concrete hard. She'd never make a decent Indian, she thought as she fell again and was hauled to her feet—I'd impale myself on my tomahawk.

Once in the cluster of trees, she leaned against a twisted thick bole and watched as Vic pulled a lighter out and began a search among the branches for their prize. Like a crazed butterfly, the flame darted and stopped, lowered, hastened toward and away from her. Every few seconds she was able to glimpse Vic's flushed face: an eye here, the mouth there. It was, finally, unnerving, and she pushed away from the tree and moved to stand by him.

"What's the matter, kid?" he said, handing her the lighter and grabbing at a low branch. Before she had time to answer, he had yanked himself up and leaves fell to her head and shoulders.

"What are you, Tarzan?" she called up.

"Confound it, woman," he said, puffing, "do you want that prize or not?"

She laughed and rested a hand against the trunk. When it was obvious the tiny lighter flame wouldn't do him much good, she held it at arm's length and looked around as best she could, seeing only a low mound in the center of the trees covered with dead leaves and branches and a few small stones. She puzzled at it for a moment, then turned her attention elsewhere, suddenly straightening. "Hey, Tarzan, can you see anything from up there?"

"Oh sure, I can see all the way to Denver. How am I supposed to be able to see anything, idiot. You've got the lighter."

"Oh. Sorry." She pulled her collar closer to her neck. If she had heard something—and she wouldn't have sworn that she did—it was probably some fieldmouse fleeing the noise they were making. A broken twig dropped on her head and she jumped, scolded herself and tried not to turn around again.

A snap. Two. One to her left, the other on her right.

"Vic?"

A third ahead of her, a fourth behind. Outside the grove, in the field.

"Vic, are you all right?"

A leaf brushed against her cheek and she slapped at it. The night's chill deepened and the lights from the highway seemed more like glowing globes of hazed ice. She wanted to flick on the lighter but was suddenly afraid to let her position be known.

Another leaf clung to her hair. When she grabbed it, it crumpled dryly and she fought to keep panic from making her choke.

Again: to the left, the right, behind, and in front.

Whispers.

"Vic, get down here now!"

She listened and heard with immense relief the scraping of leather against bark. A dark figure broke from the branches and landed lightly in front of her. A hand to her shoulder.

"Vic?"

"Who else? And why are we whispering?"

"Listen."

The distant grumbling of a truck.

"I—"

She put a hand to his mouth, felt his lips move then become still as the whispers grew louder and the footfalls came closer. His hand pressed down until she was forced into a crouch, wondering why he just didn't call out or pick up a stick and clobber whoever was stalking them.

A light flashed.

Explosive, and soaring.

A yellow-gold miniature sun that rose over the trees and gave birth to hell's shadows. She gasped, heard Vic swear under his breath. Another, and another until there were eight, perhaps more, of the gleaming things in the air over the trees.

"What . . . ?" Vic said, then yelled and yanked Dale off her feet and away from their tree. The flames were coming down, scattering in the grove. One landed precisely where they'd been standing, and she saw it was an arrow wrapped with cloth and set afire. Frowning, she moved toward it, scurried back when the others landed randomly and cracked. Three or four, she couldn't be sure, were instantly extinguished, but the rest had landed in brush or patches of dried grass. The flames caught quickly, moving away from the arrows like spreading brilliant water. Vic's hand tightened and she looked up, saw another group flurry into the air, flaming, sparking into stars before they dropped to the earth. Made immobile by shock and incomprehension, they stared as the fire torches landed and spread their flames to join those already down. Within moments they were surrounded by a low wall of fire that moved inward toward the center of the grove.

As if it were alive, she thought before something struck her on the back and dropped her to her knees. She cried out, heard Vic grunt and fall prone beside her. She leaned over, and there was an explosion at the back of her head. She fell, rolled over, and thought for a moment how nice it was that the ground was so warm, so comfortable after the cold night they'd gone into.

There was light now, weaving shadows across Vic's face, turning the trees overhead into writhing things that grasped for the light, caught it and became torches themselves. Smoke rose, stung, lay mistlike over the dead grass. She wanted to yield to the pain in her skull, to let the sleep come that nudged at her eyes. It would be nice. To sleep now. In front of the fire.

She closed her eyes, saw the cloud and the face and the water she walked.

She screamed.

Sat up and looked down at Vic. There was a black-red gleam of blood across his forehead. Quickly, she put a hand to his throat and felt the pulse, and began to gently slap his cheeks, rub the back of his neck while the flames grew as tall as she and moved closer still. She saw the mound, wondered if standing on it would give them some protection, knew she was delirious, and shook her head until the renewed pain cleared it.

She called out, demanding help, then pleading. Tears born of the smoke blinded her. She rubbed them away and choked when a breeze forced her to inhale the acrid fumes.

Wildly she reached above her and snatched a low branch to haul herself to her feet. Then she grabbed at Vic's shoulders and tried to pull him away. She grunted, couldn't move him, straightened, and spun on her heels in a tight, frantic circle. She realized there was no place to take him, that the fire had completely surrounded them, had climbed the trees and was already dropping brittle twigs like comets with sparks for tails. The breeze returned and for a blessed moment the air was clear, the flames held back. She took a deep breath, knelt again, and saw Vic's eyelids fluttering. She shouted in his ear, yanked at his coat until, dazed, he sat up and held his face in his hands. No time, she thought desperately, and tugged at his arm until he looked up, his eyes widening, his mouth opened when understanding broke through. With Dale's help he struggled to his feet, shaking his head, wiping the blood clear with a swipe of his sleeve.

Dale watched him anxiously, choked, and knew the flames were not only moving nearer, they were robbing her of much-needed air.

She stopped crying.

There was peace. A calm wave that steadied her nerves. She was rather disappointed that her life didn't flash before her eyes as it had in so many of the books she had read, the films she had seen. Not that it was worth reviewing one more time, but it was after all the only one that she had.

A roar—the fire an animal that had sensed its prey.

Sparks landed on her face. She smelled burning wool and looked down to see the hem of her coat smoldering at her knees. She slapped at it, suddenly panicking again, then slid the garment off her shoulders and trampled it until Vic spun her around and pointed.

"Over there!" he shouted over the voice of the fire.

She squinted through the billowing smoke, saw a section where the flames had already burned themselves out. Between that free area and her, however, was a low line of fire moving inexorably toward them. She looked to Vic, then shouted when a tree toppled, raining sparks and burning twigs over their heads. Too dry, too fast, she thought as Vic stripped off his coat. No wonder it moves so quickly.

A siren. Two. It seemed like hundreds.

Vic wrapped her coat around her and covered her head. She struggled, suffocating from the heat and lack of air. Then there was cloth around her bare legs and she was lifted and cradled, Vic's face close to hers.

"A good thing you're not Bella," he shouted, and began running. She closed her eyes after one glimpse up to see a nightmare of twisted branches in flames. He stumbled and she screamed, pressed closer and grabbed at his shirt. His coat fell and her legs flared in a bath of licking agony.

Then, as suddenly as it had begun, it was over.

Vic lowered her to her feet, held her tightly. A patrol car was jouncing over the field, followed closely by several fire trucks and private cars. The heat on her face, the cold at her back. She shivered and watched the orchard fall in upon itself while fire- and policemen and not a few others scurried at the perimeter, beating out the isolated patches that had fired from sparks. An ambulance pulled up behind them and two attendants took their arms and led them, unprotesting, to sit on a stretcher they'd set by the rear doors. A breath of oxygen from an inhalator, and Dale shook them off. They persisted, however, and one knelt by her legs and spread a light, cooling balm over the knives that lanced her.

He spoke to her. She couldn't hear him. She was deafened by the fire, the sirens, the shouts and, drifting above it all, the constant static of wind-blown whispers.

# CHAPTER
# VI

Chief Stockton sat on the edge of his desk, and Dale couldn't help the feeling she was playing out the same scene over. This time, however, Vic was standing behind her chair, his hands firm on her shoulders.

"It's late, Chief," he said, not bothering to hide his disgust at the official proceedings that kept them in the station. "Dale is worn out. I am worn out and my head hurts. I don't really understand what more you want from us."

Stockton frowned. "I have this itch," he said.

"I don't care about your itch," Dale muttered, and Vic squeezed quickly.

"I have this itch," the chief repeated, "that I can't find to scratch. For example," and he lifted a sheet of paper, flicked at it with his thumb. "There's no reason why that fire should have spread so rapidly.

The weeds and grass were dry and mostly dead, it's true, but there's no evidence of any flammable material that would have sparked them like that. Yet you two were trapped inside a circle, nearly burned to death.''

"No kidding," Dale said, but she was ignored.

"And you say you saw at least a dozen burning arrows. But we found none of them. Not a single one."

"Well, what you found and what we saw," Vic said angrily, "or rather, what you didn't find should have been there. We saw them. We were there, Abe, and you weren't!"

"Sure, of course you were," Stockton said in a half-hearted attempt to calm him. "But that doesn't necessarily mean that what you saw was exactly what happened. You can argue until you're blue in the face, son, but we did not find any flaming arrows, any pieces of flaming arrows or feathers or anything else." He glanced at the ceiling, pursed his lips. "And you did say you were at Elizabeth Provence's house just before. A party, is that right?"

Neither of them said a word. Dale already knew the chief thought they'd been drinking too much.

"Isn't it possible," the policeman continued, "that you climbed that tree to get your . . . apple, I think it was, and Dale was holding the lighter—the one we found in the ashes—and something startled her and she dropped it?"

"Sure, it's possible," Vic said, "but that's not the way it happened. And"—with his voice rising—"you said before the flames couldn't have spread without any artificial help, and you didn't find any of that, either."

"Right," Stockton agreed. "Which is why I have this itch." To the ceiling again, then staring at a point just in front of Dale's feet. "I, uh, don't know how to put this delicately, you two, but is it possible that for one reason or another you're not telling me exactly what went on between you two out there in that orchard?"

The implication was so ridiculous that Dale almost laughed aloud. Yet Stockton did not apologize, nor did he smile.

"Let me help you," Vic said, the strain of his anger forcing the words out slowly. "What you're trying to say—so delicately, I might add—is that Dale and I, drunk and stumbling around in the dark, made passionate love to each other while Dale dropped the lighter, the grass caught fire and we were surrounded before we ever knew what happened. That would account for the time it took for us to become trapped, and why we insist on concocting a fantastic story about flaming arrows straight out of the raids on Fort Apache. We were so caught up in ardor that we didn't even know we were about to be charred. That is what you're saying, isn't it?"

When Stockton coughed loudly and moved stiffly back to his chair, Dale shrugged Vic's hands from her shoulders and jumped to her feet. She leaned against the desk and glared until the chief was forced to look up. "I don't believe you, Abe, I really don't. I thought you knew me better than that. Well, listen, I am not a bloody common whore no matter what you think! And I sure don't go climbing around dead trees all liquored up and lifting my skirt for the first man who looks at me!"

"Dale, for God's sake," Vic warned.

But she would have none of it. She slammed a palm onto the desk. "Stockton, if you don't believe what we've told you, then you'd better put us in your two-bit jail or let us go!"

She glared, watching with pleasure the fury turning Abe's face an unpleasant red. His breathing became labored and his left hand crumpled a piece of paper blindly. Then he rose, slowly, and Dale backed away only when he came back around the desk and stood in front of her.

"Miss Bartlett, if you insist on sticking to that idiotic story of yours, there's not much I can do. The Armstrong farm has been deserted property for almost as long as you've been alive, and there's no one around who can press charges for the damage done tonight. I could, and with good cause, lock you both up on counts of malicious mischief—"

"You are crazy," Vic said.

"—but I don't think I will. Besides the fact that only a few trees were burned and so nothing major done, I knew your parents and know that you yourself don't generally behave this irresponsibly. I don't think it would be in your best interest to spend a night in our jail. Now, if there's anything more you wish to say, please let the sergeant at the desk know. Our discussion is finished."

"Anything more," Dale said slowly. "Well, believe me, there's definitely a lot more—"

"No, Dale!" Vic said, grabbing her arm and tugging her to the door. "This man has made his point, and we've made ours. Let's get out of here before he thinks of something beautiful to lock us up with."

They stood in the corridor, Dale trembling in her anger and searching the walls for something she could use as ammunition. The lights were dimmed, and as they headed toward the front their shadows were barely visible.

"A couple of hours and it'll be dawn," Vic said. "How are your legs?"

Until he mentioned it, Dale had been feeling nothing more than a generalized aching. Now, however, the pains became localized: the throbbing of her skull where the rock had struck it, a light burn on the heel of her left hand, the myriad scrapes and burns, small and digging, scattered along her legs from calf to thigh. The salve administered by the ambulance attendant had worked somewhat, but the residual stinging made her wish for a bathtub jammed with ice, or a snowbank she could fall into up to her neck. Walking, then, was a chore, but she was thankful she had worn a skirt and not her slacks; the cloth rubbing against her legs would have been too much to take—the overcoat was bad enough.

When Vic repeated his question, she shrugged her reply. "At least my headache can't be as bad as yours." She touched at the bandage wrapped round his head, remembering the gleam of black blood in the light of the fire. "Can I get something for you?"

His laugh was short and bitter. "Yeah, a new place to live. When dear landlady Emma hears I've been carousing in the fields with a nymph, she's going to want to hang me from the highest tree at the top of the park. After, that is, she tosses me out on my suitcase."

They stopped just before entering the front room.

Here the lighting was bright, and Dale squinted until her eyes adjusted while the talk of headaches and landladies faded into the ringing of the desk telephone, the bark of the sergeant's answering. She wanted to ask Vic about the fire, the whispers, the arrows that had vanished. But this didn't seem like the appropriate place; and the more she thought about it, the more she wondered just how badly that champagne had affected her. Enough to befuddle her senses? Had she been, if not drunk, then so much more than gently high that her memories were colliding, merging, and the things she had seen only fragments of things which had gone before? She denied it. The rocks that had stunned them had been thrown and were not imaginary, nor were the burns on her skin.

"Come on, Dale," he said, taking her arm and pulling her close.

They walked outside where they found Vic's car waiting, the engine running. Warmth, she thought, and slid into the front seat eagerly, hugged herself and wished she had the kindness of heart to give her coat to Vic—his had fallen into the fire and, she knew, saved her legs from worse injuries than they already suffered.

"Where?" he asked. "Home?"

"No," she said immediately. "Not yet, anyway. Just . . . just ride around for a bit, okay? Do you mind?"

He drove up to Williamston Pike, then headed east past the park and into the darkness of overhanging trees broken only by high stone walls and faintly glowing amber that marked the driveways of the Station's estates. There was no traffic and he let the car slow so her eyes could pick out the branches, the individual stones, the scurrying red eyes of creatures disturbed.

But though her eyes picked them out, she didn't see them. Rocks and fire: what had happened was a deliberate attempt to murder her. It had to be that, though she didn't know why. And there was nothing she could do about it officially because Stockton was convinced—and with reason, she reluctantly admitted—she and Vic had been merely gamboling in the meta-phorical hay, with too much drink in them to realize what was happening.

She could do nothing officially. But she didn't have to ask to know that Vic wasn't going to let this die peaceably, either. The question was: what were they going to do about it, and how?

"I'll bet you're thinking of apple pie," Vic said suddenly.

"Creep," she said.

"You know, it's funny," he said quietly, almost unheard over the thrum of the engine, "but you never think things like this are going to happen to you. You see it in the movies and you watch it on TV, you read it in the papers and you think it's all a fake, a charade to keep the masses happy. Vicarious thrills and all that business. It never happens to you, you know."

"It doesn't," she agreed.

"But it does. Has." He slapped at the steering wheel, less in anger than frustration. "And I don't figure it, Dale, really I don't. I mean . . . but I don't know what I mean!"

"I do," she said, staring at the headlights graying

the night. "It's like they say in those films you mentioned: who are your enemies? Who wants you dead?"

"Ridiculous. We're not gangsters. We wouldn't know one if we fell over him. For crying out loud, Dale, how can you make deadly enemies running a toy store?"

She didn't know.

"And me," he continued, his voice almost pleading. "I may have failed a student or two in my time, here and there around the East where I've worked . . . but to have one of them come back to burn me alive for that?" He shook his head. "No. I can't believe that."

"Vic, what happened to the arrows?"

They were silent, then, because neither had an answer. She considered the possibility that some of the onlookers had made off with some souvenirs or two, that perhaps the firemen still at the scene keeping watch over the smoldering remains would find something to lend credence to their story. But though she had no proof, she knew nothing would turn up. No arrows. No fuel. And there couldn't have been that or she would have smelled it being spread around her.

*As if it were alive*, she remembered, thinking about the fire; and she suppressed that fancy instantly, though not without a shudder.

"I know something else that's funny," she said.

"Tell me quick! I need a laugh."

"We were the only ones out looking for an apple. If we weren't, we wouldn't have been alone out there."

"So? Everyone had a different list. We just happened to pick one with apples on it."

"Coincidence?"

He reached out to turn up the heater.

"It couldn't have been, Vic. Not if we were supposed to die." She straightened, lifted her head from the back of the seat. "Vic, we were supposed to die by fire."

"I know," he said. "Otherwise we could have been nailed any time while we were running around."

"Of course, it could have been a prank that backfired, if you'll excuse the expression."

He said nothing, and she didn't press him. Yet she wanted to, desperately, to press him and make him convince her she just wasn't playing with nightmares that came to her while she was awake. It was, on the face of it, completely insane, so much so that she considered seriously accepting Stockton's skeptical version of their near-fatal accident—if only because she didn't want to scream.

"Hey," he said. "Dale, wake up."

She blinked, grinned stupidly when she realized she'd fallen into a light doze. They were parked in front of her house, and though she wanted to tell him she was too tired to walk, he helped her from the car, brought her inside, and stayed only long enough to see that she could take care of herself.

"Listen," he warned on the doorstep, "don't try to come in on Monday if you don't feel well, okay? Bella and I can handle everything. I promise you we won't drive you out of business for at least two days."

"Vic—"

He kissed her, long, gently, then pushed her inside. "It's going to sound silly maybe, but we have to have time to think. I'm getting too confused, and you must be, too. When I can think straight we'll get to the bottom of this stuff."

"But suppose—"

"Another accident? I don't think so. It would be too soon after and then the police would know for sure we were telling the truth. I have a feeling that whoever is playing with us doesn't want them to catch on. You'll be safe enough, love."

He leaned over and kissed her again, pulled the door closed. She stared at it a moment before turning and running up to her bedroom, squirming out of her clothes and scrambling into a strangely cold bed. She didn't want to close her eyes, thinking of the dreams that would take her back to the orchard and the rocks and the arrows like stars, but her resolve weakened, and the darkness was empty.

Was light.

She rolled over to look at the clock on the bureau.

"Oh my God," she said. It was nearly five in the afternoon and her stomach immediately demanded a feeding. She tossed back the blanket and sat up, carefully, the skin on her legs tight but not painful. Her headache had vanished, but there was still a hint of dizziness that kept her to the walls, holding onto furniture, the banister, clinging to her bathrobe as if that alone would prevent her from collapsing. Once in the kitchen, she downed a large glass of orange juice, then made herself coffee and a pile of toast which she took into the living room. She stifled the temptation to turn on the television, and sagged onto the sofa to eat and stare out the front window.

"Nuts," she whispered, remembering some dream-formed plan to visit the field again on her own. While the sun was up. But daylight was already veiled, the street light at the corner on and glaring. A whole day gone, she thought, amazed because she hadn't believed she was all that exhausted. Yet she had been, and now it was twilight.

She finished her coffee quickly, stood and tested her legs. There was a spot just below her left knee that felt as if it had been freshly scorched, but otherwise she was pleased to feel nothing more than a minor twinge. "Be brave, girl," she told herself and ran upstairs to dress, postponed her decision by drawing a tepid bath and soaking for nearly an hour before she grew tired of continually making it warm again. A glance in the mirror at her sleep-swollen eyes, the faint lines of weariness pulling at her mouth, and she dressed warmly in sweater and slacks, wool-lined boots, and tied a black scarf over her head.

She hesitated in the foyer, forced herself out onto the porch before she could telephone Vic for assistance. It wouldn't be fair, she decided. It wouldn't be right to drag him out again. Though he hadn't said a word, was careful about his reactions, she was positive the blow to his head had resulted in some sort of minor concussion and no matter how anxious he might be, he definitely wouldn't be up to visiting the scene of the crime in the dark.

She reminded herself to call him when she returned and order him not to report for work the next morning, then stepped down to the sidewalk.

There were six long blocks to Mainland Road, and halfway there, as she passed the police station and the town hall opposite, she wondered sourly why Oxrun's designer made those blocks so damned long. He probably rode a horse all the time, she thought, and didn't give a damn about my poor feet. But the walk surprised her by loosening her legs, and the brittle air was refreshing after the stench of last night. She estimated thirty minutes more of usable light and patted her coat pocket where she'd stuck her father's flashlight.

She grinned.

She had told herself it would be for illumination only once she reached the field, but it was heavy enough to stop anyone who attacked her if she used it right. Not, she thought, that anything was going to happen if Vic was correct—but if he wasn't . . .

She quickened her step, looking neither left nor right, staring rather at the growing row of hedge as she approached the highway. As it was late Sunday afternoon, there was little traffic in the village or on the main road, and she had no trouble crossing once she decided to make the move. Gingerly, then, she moved down and up the sides of the ditch, impatiently thrashing aside the barbed branches seeking to stop her. She stood, and took a long deep breath, as the last red glare of the setting sun faced her on the forested horizon.

She hurried, picking her way cautiously so not to turn an ankle, not looking up until she was directly in front of the orchard.

There was no one around. Firemen and police,

their tasks completed, had left earlier that morning. Nothing was left of the night before.

She touched the heavy metal of the flashlight and was reassured.

It was a bleak scene, then, as dusk turned the October light to a grainy haze. All the trees she had climbed as a child were blackened, most raped of their weakest branches, several lying forlornly on their sides. Where the firehoses had been directed there was a coating of ice, in some places thick casings that preserved in deep white the destruction of the fire. Someone not from Oxrun would call this a place of stark beauty, she thought, but the red of the sun was too much like blood.

A half-dozen ravens not yet gone for the winter had settled on the perimeter of the scene of the burning, but none of them seemed to want to venture inside. Dale watched them as they scurried in tight circles, agitated because something prevented them from satisfying their curiosity. So talk already, she told them silently, and tell good old Dale what's bothering you. But the large birds only grew more excited and suddenly, without warning, flew off as if startled by a shot.

All right, then, she thought, and began to walk, keeping to the outside of the charred area as the birds had done, peering into the orchard's remains, examining every inch of ground she passed over. The ravens returned, flew low over her head, and wheeled off, screaming. She pulled out the flashlight and followed the tight beam, kneeling every few feet to brush her hand across the ground and sweep debris away, to brush aside a twig or a small blackened stone. Once, she came upon the body of a fieldmouse evidently suffocated by the smoke. She felt tears and took up a sharp rock, dug a hole in the resisting earth and buried it, touching the small black mound with her palm while she wept silently. More quickly, then, until she had made the turn three times about the circumference and stepped back sighing.

A tree. She wished for a tall tree to climb because she knew without the seeing that the flames had burned out a near-perfect circle before stopping, though with the breeze that had been blowing they should have spread farther, more raggedly into the field. She sniffed the air, found no lingering remains of gasoline or oil; she rubbed her hand over blackened grass and smelled her fingers—nothing but the stench of fire gone cold.

And then, at the point where she had buried the mouse, she moved into the destruction. Stiff blades crumpled beneath her boots, ash lifted lazily into the air and fell behind her as if gravity had been nullified. She tried not to touch any of the trees or sagging branches, but streaks of charcoal streaked her overcoat nonetheless.

Here, she thought, is where I stood when Vic did his first looking; and here's the tree he climbed, and the mound I saw with the lighter. Oblivious to the stains, the grit, the burning of patches of ice, she crawled on hands and knees in hopes of locating a bloodstained rock—but there was nothing, nothing at all. Neither did she uncover the scorched remains of any of the arrows that had ignited the conflagration. And finally, when it was too dark to see beyond the glow of the flashlight, she gave it up and kicked furiously at a fallen trunk.

"It happened!" she said loudly, not caring if anyone was near enough to hear her. "I know it! It happened right here!"

She jabbed the light at the trees around her. Flashes, then, of fingered branches, gutted boles, thick-stemmed icicles like petrified moss. She stamped to the mound and swept it clear of debris, picking up uncovered stones and flinging them wildly into the dark. And raised a fist to the moon.

She calmed.

Wept.

Stood with a weight at her shoulders, staring until she realized she was looking at what was left of the coat Vic had wrapped around her legs before carrying her out. She knelt, poked at the few pieces of material and picked up four cold-metal buttons.

I'll get him a new one and sew these on, she thought, kicked at the rubble and dislodged a stone.

She stood, glanced down and in the flashlight glow, saw that what she had uncovered wasn't a stone.

"Oh Willy," she said. "Oh, my poor Willy."

# CHAPTER
# VII

A thin cloud poked a gray finger at the face of the moon. In the distance, the quarreling of the ravens.

Dale sat on the mound in the orchard and toyed with the flashlight. After her initial outburst at her find, she forced herself to recall as much of that day when Willy had drowned as her memory would allow. She saw Fred Borg take something from the dead boy's hand. But she couldn't make herself see it clearly. Connection via imagination, she wondered, and without conscious effort remembered a similar thing at the scene of Dave's horrid accident.

"No," she said. "It's not even coincidence because nothing's the same."

She rose, dusted futilely at her coat, and left the orchard, stumbling several times before reminding herself to turn on the flashlight before she broke a leg. At the hedge, however, she waited until Mainland was cleared of traffic before she burst through and stood on the highway shoulder, staring down the deserted length of Chancellor Avenue. No cars to distract her, no pedestrians that she could see. She wanted to run, to race the night home, but enforced tension steadied her, made her cross the road slowly and reach the sidewalk without quickening a step. A bracing breath, then, and she proceeded as if nothing at all was churning up nausea in her stomach, nothing was squirting acid into her mouth that she had to spit into the gutter or gag on. As she passed the Provence home she was glad to see all its lights were out; otherwise, and she cursed it, the temptation to stop and show the woman what she had found would have been too great. Not that Liz would have understood, or believed, but her famed cynicism might be what was needed to still the terror squirming to be released. Not Liz, then. Vic. The logical one to contact now. But again a doubt. The image of his slightly glazed eyes, the stifled pain that slid a barely controlled mask over his expression—he said he needed time to think, to sort out the confusion, and she knew it was because of the blow he took. His thoughts were scrambled, would tend to be illogical and definitely not what she . . . they needed right now.

Leave him, she thought. Let him rest.

Besides, she had to have a few minutes more to do some thinking on her own, to thrash through her wondering into speculation, and from speculation to fact. The first thing, then, was to change her clothes so she wouldn't look to the world like a chimney sweep just home from a day's grimy work. A shower to wash body and mind so she would at least have the illusion of feeling better, even if the facts didn't point that way.

She gazed over at the police station, at the single small globe over the double doors. A patrol car, empty, was parked at the curb. Stockton wouldn't be there now, and though she hesitated before continuing, she decided not to take a chance asking if Fred was on duty. There would be more questions, and a note left for the chief to read in the morning. A note that would lead to his calling, still more questions, and her lying.

Those infernal tangled webs, she thought with a silent groan; and then she groaned aloud as she approached her house and saw the dark figure hurrying down her front steps. At first she thought it was Abe out of uniform before she stared through the inadequate street lighting, recognized the woman and tried to decide which way to turn to escape a meeting. But it was too late.

The woman hurried toward her. Her face was harshly lined, obscuring a youthful attractiveness which had become frozen in years-long bitterness. The hair pulled back and bunned was too gray to be brown, too brown to be aged. There was no make-up that could have softened the overhanging nose, the jutting cleft chin, the bloodless lips between.

"I was coming to see you," Milly Campbell said, her voice remarkably similar to her aunt's. "You weren't home." Almost an accusation.

"I was out for a walk," Dale explained, and regretted it immediately. Milly glanced over the soot and ash that clung to her coat, face, and hands.

"I heard about the fire, you see, and I wanted to

bring you something in case you were hurt. In the fire, you see.''

In her hands was a small, foil-covered bowl she thrust at Dale, who took it before it dropped to the sidewalk. She felt its warmth and shifted it to hold against her side. "Well, I'm really grateful, Milly, thank you. And really, I'm all right. I just got a slight knock on the noggin and a couple of small burns that only hurt when I laugh.''

Milly didn't move from the middle of the walk. Her hands were jammed into her black coat pockets, her eyes steady on Dale's. "You shouldn't have been there, maybe,'' she said. "Them's dangerous fields there at night they tell me.''

Dale smiled. "To my eternal regret I found that out the hard way. Never again, believe me.''

They stared at each other until Milly finally swallowed, wavered and took a step back. "Well, as long as you're not badly hurt, that you're doing well in spite of the fire . . .''

"Oh, please!'' Dale said suddenly. "Won't you come in and sit for a minute or two? It's a long walk home, and getting to be winter cold. Maybe you'd like a cup of coffee or tea to warm yourself up a bit?''

Milly shook her head, her expression unchanging. "No, but thank you anyway. My aunt is alone and I should be back.'' She stretched out a hand, drew it back quickly and walked away.

"Are you sure, Milly?'' Dale called after her. "It won't be any trouble at all, honestly.''

There was no answer. Dale became rigid as she fought the impulse to chase after the Campbell woman, grab her thin shoulders and shake her until something that made sense broke through those tightly cold lips. She couldn't understand, and hated not understanding what the Campbell family found so urgent that they had to be continually solicitous of her welfare. First the aunt and now the mother, and the tears she had seen in Dave's eyes the day he was killed in the crash. If none of her own, though admittedly not close, friends had bothered to pay her a call, why these near strangers? What, she wondered as she unlocked the front door, was there about her that elicited the good Samaritan in those gloomy Scots?

It was a speculation that might have taken up the rest of her evening, but she reminded herself that she already had planned a visitation of her own. After a quick gulp of tepid coffee, she showered and changed and was out of the house before its warmth could trap her into napping on the sofa or taking an hour to talk with her plants.

She walked briskly, her arms swinging, her head straight. March, you fool, she grinned at herself, skipped a few paces to break the martial rhythm she'd fallen into, and laughed. A few minutes later she was up and across the Pike and heading west until she reached Northland Avenue. The streets that extended over the Pike on this side of the park from the center of town did so for only a single block before being stopped by a tall hurricane fence that separated the village from the sprawling expanse of the Oxrun Memorial Park. She never understood how some people could live so close to a cemetery, but shrugged off the morbidly gathering ideas of answers and counted two houses in before coming to a halt.

It was a small and game attempt at a modern ranch that failed miserably because of the Victorian monsters that flanked it, backed it, faced it across the street. A yellow light glowed over the plain front door, and in the picture window to its right red drapes dimmed a lamp set behind them. A skeletal dogwood too close to the walk made her swerve onto the lawn, and the early frost crackling beneath her shoes snapped at her nerves and she almost jumped onto the concrete just to bring back the silence.

She waited. Heard nothing inside. Licked at her lips and, keeping her hand in her pocket, knocked loudly on the door. When it opened, she didn't wait for an invitation but hurried over the threshold and into the light.

The room was as she had expected, though she didn't know exactly why. A single worn couch, a matching armchair with an ashtray stand beside it; no television or sign of a radio, the walls shelved and packed with what could easily have been hundreds of books and back issues of professional magazines and journals. On the long wall at the side of the house was a fireplace topped with a wood mantel, stark and completely utilitarian.

The wall-to-wall carpeting was a dull, lifeless green, and in its center, Jaimie McPherson was sitting with a chessboard between his legs. He looked up, waved when he saw who had entered, and returned to his game. Dale was forgotten.

But she was pleased to see that Ed was startled by her unannounced appearance. He fumbled with her coat, rushed to hang it in a hall closet. Like a kid trapped in the pantry, she thought grimly.

"Dale," he finally managed to get out, guiding her quickly to the chair, "I thought you were . . . well, when I heard about what happened, I would have thought you'd be hospitalized or something."

"Word travels fast," she said flatly. "It only happened last night."

Ed took his place on the couch, Jaimie directly at his feet. "Well, I must admit I tried to call you a little while back. To see about those dreams of yours." He took off his glasses and pointed with them. "I do worry about you now and then, you know."

"Well, thank you," she said.

The door was behind her, the couch serving as a break between living room and dining area. Directly in front of her was the fireplace, and on the mantel the chess set that Dave Campbell had made. She glanced around the room, at the shelves she could see, then back to the mantel.

"My expensive stare." He laughed quickly.

"I thought you wanted it as an addition to your collection. I don't see any others."

"I like to keep it out. I don't use it, of course. Jaimie and I use that plastic one he has when he beats me."

"I don't beat you, Father," the boy said without looking up.

"No, of course not," Ed said shortly. "But you have come close on occasion, you have to admit."

"Sure, Father," Jaimie said. He kept his eyes on the board.

Out of sight in the dining room area a grandfather

clock chimed in Westminster the hour, and after the
eighth peal had faded, Ed crossed his legs and replaced his glasses. In leather-patched tweed jacket
and turtleneck shirt, he seemed more a man posing
for a magazine profile than someone spending a quiet
night home with his son. Dale was reminded of
Elinor McPherson's death, and she tried without success to place Ed in the role of dual parent; from the
way the boy spoke to his father, he evidently had
most things his way, and Ed seemed not to offer him
much, if any, resistance at all.

She smiled. With one hand smoothed the collar of
her blouse over the light sweater she'd worn—a dark
green to highlight what blond her hair showed that
evening.

"Is it cold out?" Ed asked finally, nodding to her
sweater, then to the closet.

"It's not summer any more, that's for sure," she
said, her smile more broad. "I wouldn't be surprised
if we had a good fall of snow before Thanksgiving."

Ed grunted, watched his son move a Norman queen.
He leaned forward, looked up to Dale, and shrugged
as if to indicate that his son didn't need his help,
especially when it hadn't been requested. He straightened, coughed into a fist, and lay a hand across the
back of the couch. "And what, then, brings you to
my side of town, Dale? A friendly visit, I hope?"

"Now why would it be otherwise, Ed," she said,
and lifted her fist from her lap. "But I found something tonight. At the field where the fire was. Where
I was almost killed."

"Jaimie," he said abruptly, "would you mind

excusing us?" When the boy didn't move, he added sternly, "Now, if you please."

Jaimie took his time standing, nodded once toward Dale, and moved slowly, almost disdainfully, down the short hall. Dale looked over her shoulder, saw a light flare, cut off by a door closed carefully.

"He gets moody sometimes," Ed explained with a hint of apology. "I don't like to disturb him with such . . . unpleasant talk."

"Commendable," she said.

"But you mentioned that you had found something tonight. What is it? And why did you bring it to me?"

"Well," she said, opening her fingers, "because I think this belongs to you."

He seemed at first unconcerned until Dale realized he couldn't see clearly. She stretched out her hand. McPherson squinted, rose, and gingerly took the object from her palm. She couldn't tell whether or not he was only being careful, or afraid of it.

"I don't remember all the names," she said, "but isn't that one of the pawns supposedly representing the Hound of Something or other?"

"Culann," Ed said. He held the chessman to his eyes, turned it slowly and shook his head. Dale rose, then, and took the piece from him. His fingers groped, and relaxed. When he didn't speak, she took the board down from the mantelpiece and placed it on the carpet. Kneeling, she set the pawn on its space and looked up.

"At the scene of the fire, Ed. How did it get there?"

The analyst seemed stunned. Again he removed

his glasses, this time setting them on a cushion of the sofa. He sat heavily, and rubbed the sides of his nose with two fingers, tugged at his shock of hair, rubbed his nose again.

"Come on, Ed," she prompted, "it's yours. I'd like to know how it got into the field."

His eyes wandered, snapped back into focus and his expression hardened. "Are you suggesting, Dale, that I had something to do with what happened? That I set fire to that place while you were out there, you and Blake? Is that what you're suggesting?"

She sat back on her heels, her hands covering her knees. "It just seems odd to me, Ed, that such a fragile and valuable piece of workmanship should somehow find its way into a field; and not only a field, but one where there just happened to be an awfully big fire last night." She raised a palm to quiet his sputtering protest. "I don't like what I'm saying either, Ed, but you're going to have to do a lot of explaining to prove to me it wasn't more than a simple coincidence."

Once more she saw the dazed look, as though he had suddenly found himself in a room he'd never seen before, speaking with someone whose language didn't at all resemble the one he spoke. But as before, his face cleared. He pushed himself off the couch and strode to the hall entrance, calling his son, his anger barely controlled. And when the light from the boy's room spilled into the corridor, Dale snatched up the board and replaced it on the mantel, turned just as he followed his father into the center of the room.

"Jaimie," Ed said, taking the boy's shoulders and

turning him to face her, "Miss Bartlett here found something of mine today, something in a place where it shouldn't have been. Something, in fact, that never should have left this house in the first place. Jaimie, do you have any idea what I'm talking about?"

Jaimie's freckles seemed to deepen as he paled. He lowered his gaze to stare at a foot that was toeing a groove in the carpet.

"Jaimie!"

She saw the man's hands tighten, the boy wince without making a sound. Then he looked from side to side, sullenly admitting his guilt. "I was playing," he said softly.

"What?"

"I said I was playing, okay?"

"Monsters?" Dale suggested, thinking of the toys he liked to purchase, the robots he would build with the construction kits he had been collecting recently.

Jaimie looked up at her hopefully, saw no anger, and smiled. "Yes, ma'am, that's what it was all right. The . . . the piece is a good one, you know. Scary and all. So when the police left there this afternoon, I played around the place where it had been burned. Then this man comes back, some man in a uniform and he yelled at me and I got scared so I ran away before he could catch me. I . . . I forgot the piece. I"—and he turned to his father—"I was going back to get it. Honestly, Father, I was. I wasn't going to leave it out there. Willy's father made it. I wasn't going to leave it."

"Jaimie, I've told you a thousand times you're not . . ." Ed stopped, exasperated, sending a weak apologetic smile in Dale's direction. "Jaimie, just go to your room, please. We'll talk about this later. When we're alone.''

"Yes, Father."

"Jaimie," Ed said when the boy started for his room, "what do you say, son?"

Jaimie brushed a hand through his hair, tucked a thumb into his belt. "Good night, Miss Bartlett. I'm sorry I caused you any trouble."

"Don't worry about it," she said. "You didn't." And she hoped her smile showed more warmth than she felt.

"Well, then," Ed said heartily, clapping his hands once and rubbing his palms briskly as he went to the mantel and adjusted the board slightly. "Well! Dale, I don't know how to thank you. It's a miracle the Hound wasn't stolen, or lost forever in that dreadful place. Thank heavens he wasn't playing there yesterday with it, or it might have been burned beyond repair."

"That's quite all right," she said. "Now I think I'd better get my coat and be off, if you don't mind."

Ed nodded, fetched her coat and, as he opened the door, restrained her with a touch to her arm. "Dale, do you think that's enough of a coincidence for you?"

She opened her mouth to apologize, shut it and contrived to look properly foolish. For a moment she thought he was going to pat her on the head, and to avoid it, she hurried off the stoop and down to the sidewalk. At the corner she glanced back over her shoulder and saw him still standing in the doorway. She wanted to wave, but crossed over the Pike instead and headed toward home. She scarcely felt the rising wind as it sought the openings at her neck and wrists, dipped under the coat, and made her shiver. Had she the nerve, she would have waited a few minutes and then sneaked back to stand under the front window. She wanted very much to hear the conversation between Ed and his son, and wondered which one would be doing all the yelling. The abrupt change in roles was too unsettling for her to believe it was the way things actually existed in that household. From the rudely disinterested to the quivering contrite was too many degrees of contrast from what she had seen; and she didn't believe for a minute that Jaimie was stupid enough to take something that valuable to play with in a charred field. A boy he was and most certainly prone to boyish pranks. But not this. Not Jaimie. But neither could she really convince herself that the boy had anything to do with the attempt on her life. There was no sense there, none at all.

Another gust interrupted her ruminating long enough for her to grab the scarf she'd jammed into her pocket and tie about her head. It wasn't all that helpful, but pulling it down to cover her nape and by raising the collar she was able to preserve a temporary illusion of warmth. Then she waved her hand in front of her eyes as if brushing away smoke.

During the daylight, from where she was standing, the tips of the trees on the park hill could easily be seen. Now, however, where a screen of black should have been there was a tiny ember glowing a dim yellow. It winked, was gone for nearly a minute before returning to prove she hadn't been imagining it. Her first thought instantly discarded was a star blocked by a cloud; her second that someone else was being attacked as she and Vic had been, only this time within the confines of the park. It wasn't until she had run a full block that she remembered Fred's complaints about the bonfires and the late night parties. It was rather cold for that now, but as she slowed to a walk, she debated detouring to the police station—it might only lead to trouble; her credibility there was none too good.

What, then? She could leave well enough alone and head straight for home to chase sleep by thinking about Ed McPherson. But home, she realized with a melancholy wrench, did not hold out much hope for comfort. A lot of empty rooms, her plants, and the television that spoke but never listened. By the time she reached the library and had turned the corner onto Park Street, the glow had vanished with the thought of her bed. And at the park's main entrance she decided it wouldn't hurt to do a little eavesdropping of her own. It was possible she might even be able to learn who those boys were who had the crush, who were sending her those notes at the store.

It was, she thought, as good an excuse as any.

The gates were set back from the fence, constructed of the same iron spears connected with crossbars top and bottom. She stood by the encased lock, staring dumbly at the heavy link chain wrapped around the bars tightly, touched it once before sighing away her conscience and leaping upward. She grabbed the crossbar and hauled herself over, her muscles and lungs protesting the sudden and unusual strain. When she landed on the tarmac walk she fell, sprawled, then sat up to face the darkened street.

Now if Vic were here, she told herself, he'd say I was being silly and childish, flirting dangerously with another brush with the already short-tempered Stockton. On the other hand, she thought as she struggled painfully to her feet, where's the law against acting silly, childish, and flirtatious?

She saluted the street and ran back into the park, following the path in its meandering. Every third street lamp was still lighted, and would be so until dawn, and she ran from spot to spot as though the glow on her back was a charm for safety. She took deep breaths in her running, felt her cheeks begin to ache pleasantly, not only from the cold that stung them but also from the grin that she couldn't be rid of; a laugh bubbled then and exploded until she reminded herself sharply that the idea of eavesdropping included remaining silent and unseen. A second quick laugh and she felt the path rising, knew she was halfway past the playing fields about even with the bandstand. She could see nothing beyond the closely packed trees and shrubs, however, walls of a vast botanical tunnel that hissed and closed silently behind her.

Fancies, she thought; not very good for spies and such like me.

And when she reached a bend that would angle her away from the hill's low summit, she stopped and grabbed at her side until her breathing became less arduous, less painful. The glow was clearly visible now, but still only a glow. Somewhere, she thought, there has to be a . . . and she bent over to search the

brush for a trail that would lead her away from the
path. As soon as she found it, she pushed through
some laurel and moved cautiously, not knowing if
the kids would bother setting up some warning system against the coming of the police. And immediately the thought came, she prayed Fred wasn't
engaged in one of his stakeouts. If she were brought
in with a group of cavorting high school students,
Abe would surely lock her up this time, no questions
and no arguments.

The glow increased, and she wished for the warmth
it implied.

When a low-hanging pine bough slapped her with
its needles, she instantly stuck out her hands, waving
them from side to side so as not to be caught again.
The moon was fading now. The trail even less friendly
and pleasant with that thin light gone, the only illumination a flickering she could see ahead and above her.
Though the wind was partially blunted by the closeness of the trees, enough sifted through to chill her,
make her teeth chatter so much she had to put a hand
to her chin to stop it. A sudden dip nearly tripped
her; a root snaking in front of her sent her silently,
sharply to her knees. Quickly she bit down on her
thumb to keep from crying out; and in waiting for the
sting to pass, she heard the voices.

Low. Insistent. Not at all the revelry she had been
expecting at some illicit party. That the sounds carried this far froze her—if she could hear them, they
probably would be able to hear her. She cursed,
shook her head angrily at herself, and began to back
away. It wouldn't be much fun, or informative, if she
couldn't get close enough to see what was going on,

but neither was she prepared to be discovered and forced into an explanation of why she was there. Besides, from the sound of it, whoever was speaking was involved in an argument; and as though in telepathic confirmation there was a briefly loud exchange and a thrashing of the bushes as someone walked rapidly toward her.

Heedless of the noise she would produce, more worried about being found, she scrambled off the trail into the protection of a low thick shrub. And as her eyes became more adjusted to the fringes of the fire's glow, she saw that the figure now standing in the trail where she had just been was a girl. A small girl. And she was joined by an equally small boy.

# CHAPTER
# VIII

"I can't understand why you're so bothered."

"We've lost another one, fool, that's why! We've lost another one."

"We had five. Now there are three. We can do as well with two, you know. One, if we have to."

The voices frightened her. The backlighted figures were clearly those of children, but the voices she heard were adult in tone; and in closing her eyes it was easy to imagine a man and a woman standing not five feet from where she crouched.

"We have five days."

"I know that. I haven't forgotten how to count."

"Well said. Can you do as well so the others won't run?"

"Run? Where are they going to run to? Back across the water? This is the best chance, the only chance we'll have for—"

"All right, all right! There's no sense in our arguing. We'll only make it worse. What's done is done. And if what you say is right, we have to do it again. Two, you say? I wouldn't like to be here if you're wrong."

A cramp knotted the back of a thigh, and she reached to massage it through her coat, gnawing on her lips to keep from crying out.

"And what of the other troubles? I don't like it. We risk too much."

"There's little we can do now to stop it."

"Then the least you can do is be a little more efficient, don't you think?"

Dale brought her arm forward again, brushing it carelessly against her coat. There was a sudden alarming clatter as the flashlight fell. The voices stopped, and she looked up to see the figures turned in her direction. Panic flooded out reason, then, and she snatched up the light and jumped to her feet. Immediately the figures took a step toward her she switched on the flash to blind them, heard their angrily startled shouts as she ran between them, striking out with her arms to knock them aside. There was no time to search for the path to the main gates now; she stumbled onward through the brush, slamming once into a bole as a warning yell rose hysterically behind her. She gasped, pushed herself faster, and broke onto the open slope. Frost had already whitened the ground and crackled like twigs beneath her feet as she ran without looking back. The wind shoved her, carried to her the distant sounds of more shouting, but though there didn't seem to be any pursuit she didn't slow until she tripped and fell onto her stomach, rolled, thrashed about until she regained her feet. Standing, then, and watching the glow at the top of the hill flare once before dying into black. Her breasts and knees ached from striking the hard earth, and her mouth gaped to find the air her lungs demanded. She turned, began a trot, angling away from the main entrance toward the park's southern boundary. Listening, always, for the footfalls that never came, the sudden cries of discovery that remained silent in the wind.

She was like an automaton—her legs moving her, her arms pumping for her, but her mind a deliberate blank. The immediate sense of fear had vanished, was slowly replaced by a giddy feeling of the sublimely ridiculous. As she passed into the trees again, she considered what she had done and wondered why—after all, they were only children up there on the hill; and though their conversation had been nonsensical in the extreme, there was nothing so threatening about it that should have caused her to run like that. What she should have done was pop up and yell surprise, what the hell are you doing here. But she hadn't. And she didn't know why.

It was a numbers game they were playing. Five to three to two to a possible one. Choosing up teams would have been the obvious answer had it been daylight, on the field, with uniforms and a ball. But at night, on the hill, with a fire that died as quickly as it took to spot it?

She reached the fence and leaned heavily against it, staring gratefully through the bars to her house across the street. There wasn't enough space for her to squeeze through, yet she felt there was no possible way she would be able to duplicate her earlier feat and clamber over the top. Her legs, her burns, the side of her head were combining into a collective agony that sprang tears to her eyes; and the stings and slashes of branches and her fall compounded the wavelike pain. The wind sought her out, scurried dried leaves around her ankles, pushed them into her face and she was too tired to brush them away. A car passed, but she couldn't think clearly enough to call out. A drop of moisture settled onto her cheek and she thought she was crying again, but a finger to her eye disproved the notion and when she looked down to the corner street light, she saw dashes of white shooting past the globe.

Snow. It was snowing; and she groaned.

An effort, she urged herself; make an effort, you idiot!

The iron was hotly cold when she grabbed at the fence. Two abortive leaps fell short of the crossbar, and she pulled herself up until one hand successfully caught the black metal ledge. She dangled for a moment, weeping with a pain that goaded her anger, whipped the other hand up to catch and haul, throw one leg up and over as her coat snared on a spearpoint and tore loudly. She straddled the bar for a few seconds' respite, too dizzy to look down, keeping her eyes on her hands as they turned to allow her to drop off on the other side. Her legs collapsed under her weight and she sprawled on the sidewalk. Then: come on, Abe, you creep, drive by and see the drunk crawling on your precious street.

The key dropped four times as she fumbled with haste and numb fingers. And four times she swore at the top of her voice, not caring if the neighbors heard her and summoned the riot police. And when the door fell inward, she stumbled over the threshold, shedding her coat to the floor and flailing her way into the living room where she dropped onto the sofa, one hand on the carpet, the other under her face.

I'm cracking up, she thought, pulling her knees up to her chest. I'm letting shadows frighten me, even when there are no shadows to be scared of.

A domineered analyst, two children who sounded like adults, and a stupid chess piece that looked like a poisoned dog—a beaut of a day, Miss Bartlett; and she decided that she didn't care what time it was, she was going straight to bed.

And in thinking, slept.

*Willy's face.*

*The cloud.*

*The green. The brown. Blending now with sparks of red and amber.*

*Willy's face. And not his face. The small boy drowned became a young man living became an old man dying became an ancient/young face that belonged neither to the boy nor the man. The hair grew long and flowing as if there was a wind—though the cloud remained—and the brow furrowed, the cheeks filled and became scarred, the chin squared and grew a beard that accentuated a broad nose and thick, mole-pocked lips. An ancient/young face that stared without anger, without joy, without expression. A stone face carved from a flesh-toned boulder.*

*The cloud moved.*

*The face remained. Still encased, yet no longer centered, higher now to expose a thick-muscled neck.*

*In the green. In the brown. In the sparks of red and amber.*

During the night her position woke her and she stumbled up the stairs and into bed. And when she awakened, she lay gazing at the stucco whorls in the ceiling, thinking about a time when she thought her life placid enough to even be called somewhat dull by those who didn't know the world in Oxrun Station. She smiled, stretched, massaged her breasts, stomach, sides. Dull. For the weekend just passed, to call that word an understatement would be an understatement in itself.

And in the light that found gaps in the curtains and made shimmering bars across her blanket, the fear she had worn like a second coat became less intense, more a fading reaction to a half-remembered nightmare. And though the sense of threat lingered, it had become edged in nebulous doubt. What she needed, she decided, was a plan, a method by which she could evaluate what had happened, what was happening. She had demanded and received at the McPhersons' a coincidence, but perhaps the coincidences of the past few months added up to something more.

"And maybe not," she said aloud, threw off the covers and padded into the bathroom. "Look at it this way," she told her reflection in the mirror over the basin, "in the cold light of day, as they say, what really happened to you, kid? You got yourself caught in a fire in Armstrong's orchard (and face it, kid, you weren't totally sober), found a chessman a kid had been using to play monster in the ashes, found a bunch of kids playing at bonfire on the hill . . .'' She shrugged. All of it was real enough—the puckering blotches on her face and legs were proof enough of that—but a connection? She turned on the shower and watched condensation fog the mirror, fade her image like a ghost at dawn. Not simply the transformation of the face in the cloud, but also the almost abrupt loss of terror which it had previously spawned. It was a curiosity now rather than an obsession, and she thought the shift might be interesting enough to report to Ed in his office.

Cleansed, then, and dressed, feeling as though the weekend had never happened except for the aches of her flight, she hurried down to the store, found she was half an hour early and used the time to linger over a cup of coffee in the luncheonette.

When Bella arrived, Dale spent the first few minutes assuring her there was nothing wrong, that she was indeed well and able to carry on her duties as before.

"Well . . ." Bella said doubtfully. "When I called last night and you didn't answer, I didn't know what to do. I thought you were dead, Dale, and . . ."

There were tears, the first Dale had seen Mrs. Inness shed since the death of the Bartletts. They dropped rather than flowed, one at a time without accompaniment of a sob, a catch. Dale quickly embraced her, rocking her for a minute that filled with guilt over the arguments they'd had and the near break that occurred last August. She tried patting comfort into the broad back, mumbled meaningless

sounds that carried, she hoped, a plea for the absolution she suddenly felt she needed.

"Enough," Bella said abruptly, pulling back and
tugging at her dress. "I'm a stupid old woman. I
should have known you could take care of yourself."

"If I could," Dale said as they walked back to the
storeroom, "I wouldn't have gotten into all that
trouble."

Bella stood by the yellowed sink, fussing with her
make-up in front of the cracked mirror neither had
bothered to replace. "Well, I suppose it's just as well
that it happened, dear. Now you'll learn not to be so
foolish, to watch yourself and maybe"—the side-
ways glance was sly—"find someone who can help
you."

"Bella!" Dale jammed a thumb into her side. "A
deal. No matchmaking before lunch, okay? Just this
once?"

Bella agreed reluctantly, then asked about Vic.

"You know," Dale said, "I haven't thought about
him at all this morning. My God, I expect him in
today." She frowned. "I wouldn't be surprised if he
didn't come, though. He took quite a whack on the
head."

"Well, don't call him," Bella said as Dale turned
to leave. "If he's sleeping, it's the best thing for
him. Keep him off his feet."

Dale checked her hair quickly, not answering, pulling at her sleeves as she hurried out to the counter. A
group of women burst chattering through the door,
filling the shop with inconsequential noise that seemed
to her to be like a symphony first heard and never
forgotten. Reality. Home again. And nothing had

changed, she thought behind her best professional smile. They come to see the victim, paw the boxes and try the puzzles and they'll leave without buying. She tapped a finger anxiously against the counter top. The telephone at her right hand remained silent. Twice she reached for it and twice saw Bella glaring disapprovingly at her. She was probably right, but Dale couldn't stand the incredibly slow way the hands on the wall clock moved; and she was wrong about the buying. Puzzles seemed to have enjoyed a renaissance over the weekend because by eleven there were none left on the floor and Bella was actually perspiring as she carted out what was left in the back. It was most likely another television show, Dale decided; one mention by a star, and those who had to keep up with the Hollywood Joneses flew out in force to be among the first to say that they too had whatever it was worth having.

Jaimie came in at the height of the rush, and Dale only had time to smile and receive a smile in return. It was lunch hour at the school, she realized, because soon after he was joined by Melody Forrester who cooed unashamedly at the mathematical games he showed her. Carl Booth, no slimmer after a summer-long diet, darted in behind the raven-haired Newcastle twins, and Dale began to wonder if there wasn't an impromptu convention in progress, and had to laugh behind her fist when Bella's "May I assist you young people?" was constantly ignored.

It was obvious that Jaimie hadn't received any significant punishment for the chessman episode since he was able to walk out with over twenty dollars worth of math games she was sure he had no use for.

Melody and Carl bought the same. The Newcastle twins carried off seven different books on games theory. Dale only blinked and scratched at her head— kids know too much, was her single thought; and when they had left, though adults still milled, the store seemed quieter, more somber. Bella, for one, was pleased and said so as she fought with straggles of hair that refused to stay off her forehead.

"But, Bella, they weren't teasing you this time."

"Of course they weren't. They were ignoring me completely! I tell you, Dale, that's a bad lot there. They have no respect for the older generation, none at all. Things were mighty different when I was a girl."

"I would imagine they were." Dale grinned, and left the woman to handle a customer while she stared out the window, wondering about Vic and hoping he was all right. The clouds of the previous night had dispersed before dawn, and bright sunlight flared off the windows of the shops across the street. She had to squint, finally, then grab at the edge of the window frame, nearly toppling a cardboard display of Halloween witches and goblins.

Directly in front of the store were the children. Talking. Taking their purchases from the brown paper bags and waving them about with a great deal of animation. But the glare served as a spotlight from behind, and they were momentarily in shadow before moving on, in shadow that resembled those she had seen in the park.

Now that's impossible, she thought as she straightened the display. Both the twins spoke with a pronounced lisp, and Melody's voice was irritatingly high. Jaimie she had left at home only minutes before she climbed the park gate, and Carl . . . she shook her head vigorously, prompting Bella to rush to her side.

"No, it's all right," she insisted when the older woman tried to urge her into the back room for a rest. "I was daydreaming and the light from the windows over there made me dizzy. Really, I'm okay."

"You're not, you know," Bella said, but was prevented from further comment by the intrusion of another customer.

She had thought about visiting Ed during her lunch hour to tell him about the change in the dream, but had decided to visit Vic instead to see what had happened. Now she changed her mind. All the calming rationalizations she'd developed since waking suddenly found themselves on shaky ground and she needed Ed's maddeningly professional manner to spread new balm over her aggravated nerves. She also wanted reassurance that her mind was still functioning normally.

Finally, when three people in succession failed to rouse her from her contemplation, Bella shoved her coat into her hands and ordered her politely from the store.

"Food is what you need, young lady. And after you get some, we'll try some of my special medicine in the back. You may say you're doing fine, but that weekend is catching up with you whether you like it or not. Now go, please, before the word spreads that this store is being clerked by a spook."

Dale jumped at the odd choice of words, but she

acquiesced without argument. Bella immediately helped her with the coat, set a scarf around her neck, and put her firmly out the door.

The sun was warm, the air still as she walked toward the luncheonette. A nod, a smile, and she stood at the corner curb. She didn't feel at all hungry despite Bella's prescription and, after a quick mental toss of a coin, she spun left and crossed the street and stopped two doors in from the High and Centre corner. Between a piano showroom and a teen boutique was a simple glass-and-aluminum door bearing the stark legend: Dr. E. W. McPherson. A touch to her throat to adjust the scarf and she pushed in, hurried up the dark carpeted stairs bathed in a soft white light. At the first landing was a large artificial rubber plant, silent sentinel before a paneled oak door which opened with a hiss when she trod on a narrow black mat.

The waiting room was small. A couch on the right behind a chrome coffee table, two armchairs on the left separated by a bronze ashtray stand; end tables cluttered with new magazines, and a series of nondescript landscapes on walls of a yellow so pale it was almost white. In the center of the far wall was a C-shaped desk behind which sat a woman reading a paperback novel. She was middle-aged, blond, conservatively dressed, and, from the eager way she looked up at Dale's entrance, thoroughly bored.

"Yes, may I help you?" An automatic response not quite humanized by the bright white smile that accompanied it. She leaned forward on her elbows, one hand resting on a card file, the other poised with a gilted ballpoint pen.

Dale glanced around quickly, gnawed hesitantly at her lower lip. She considered rushing back out again. The office was quiet, too quiet after her hectic morning, her harrowing weekend. She felt very small under the woman's steady gaze.

"Ma'am, are you all right?"

"The doctor," Dale said. "Dr. McPherson. I'd like to see him if I can. It's very important."

The receptionist shook her head sadly. "I'm sorry, miss . . ."

"Bartlett."

"I'm awfully sorry, Miss Bartlett, but Dr. Mc-Pherson isn't in. You're not a regular, are you?" When Dale shook her head, the woman nodded. "I thought not. I'm only a temporary, you see. Doctor's been on a leave of absence, you see, and I'm still getting regulars who've forgotten he's shifted them to Dr. Lansing over on Steuben. You do know where Steuben is, don't you?"

"Sure I do," Dale said sharply, "but what's all this about a leave of absence? I thought I was a friend of his, but I wasn't told anything about this."

The woman's smile faded. "Well, he has been out of the office for, well, nearly two weeks, you see. Or is it three? To be honest, I don't really know. I myself have been here for two, anyway. It's a great job, of course, sitting here all day answering the phone and all." She lifted her book. "I get a lot of reading done, too, but it sure does get awfully—"

"Dr. McPherson," Dale interrupted. "Has he gone anywhere?"

The receptionist blinked. "I thought you said you were his friend? You should know he hasn't gone anywhere. He's just on a leave of absence, like I said. Are you sure you don't want the other doctor's address? Dr. Lansing, I mean, I'm sure he could—''

Dale turned on her heel and left, taking the steps slowly after a long study of the office door. Leaves of absence, she had always thought, generally entailed things like graduate study programs or recuperations—Ed fit neither of these categories; and it was peculiar that he never mentioned his taking anything that resembled time off from the office. Some of his patients were surely abandoned in the midst of their therapy, and what had happened to his regular secretary? A temporary suggested the woman was let go permanently. She stopped at the foot of the stairs, pulled thoughtfully at her scarf before racing back up into the office. The receptionist was startled into dropping her book.

''Listen,'' Dale said, leaning on the desk, ''I'm sorry about that,'' and she pointed to the book, ''but I wonder if you could tell me Miss Whatshername's address. You know . . .''

''Evans?''

Dale nodded quickly. ''Right, Miss Evans. Do you know where she lives?''

The woman frowned and looked down at her hands. ''Well, I don't know if I'm supposed to—''

''I swear I won't tell. Please, what's her address?''

''Well . . . actually, she doesn't have one, you see.''

''What?''

''I mean, she doesn't have one here in town. She left. I suppose the doctor gave her notice or something. I don't know for sure. Anyway, when I came in to take over, she had everything packed away in a carton and said she was leaving. Somewhere out West, I think."

Dale turned a complete circle, stared longingly at the door to the inner office, then thanked the woman and left before questions could be asked. Back on the sidewalk she checked her watch. Bella, she decided, could hold the fort for a while; she had some prying to do that she felt couldn't wait. Walking swiftly away from the business district, she created a silent conversation to explain to Ed why she had to visit him again—an apology for the night before was the best bet; her conscience was bothering her and the need to lighten its load too pressing to ignore and too personal to handle by telephone. Ed would be properly condescending without knowing it, would surely offer no resistance in telling her where his secretary had gone. After that (the scenario progressed), she would wire the girl to learn as many of the details of Ed's last working days as she knew, and after that . . . after that . . .

"Oh, for crying out loud!" she said angrily, stopping and leaning against a telephone pole. "Dale, what are you doing?"

What she was doing, she told herself scathingly, was behaving like an empty-headed fool. In the first place, she had no logical reason for wanting Miss Evans' address—she certainly couldn't fake a friendship without Ed's catching on; secondly, if he was in fact involved in something vaguely or blatantly illegal, her sudden interest would probably caution him into stubborn silence. And most important was the distant but distinct possibility that he wasn't involved at all, that it was Jaimie who was behind whatever she thought was going on, and Jaimie was the one she had to worry about, not his father.

Her anger grew as she headed back to the store. She had gone and confused herself again, finding faint trails that seemed to lead somewhere, that led nowhere except to frustration. What she needed was Vic's cool cynicism to blow away the fog she'd created. The more she wondered about coincidences and connections, the more she doubted there was anything to wonder about—and yet things kept happening that immediately threw her into confusion again. What it was, she finally concluded, was a supposition based on an inexplicable sense of things not right, a vague and directionless feeling that somehow she was caught up in an action of which she was only peripherally aware—like a net spread across a jungle canopy, invisible, threatening, yet totally and dangerously real.

No wonder Stockton couldn't believe her story of flaming arrows and fire almost alive.

And Bella, poor Bella, was too dream-laden with fancies of matrimony.

Liz, perhaps, if she would only come out of her costumed world and join the living.

It was Vic, then, as she had known it would be, and as soon as she reached the shop she hurried back into the small storeroom/office and dialed his number.

"Well," he said, his voice tired, fighting to sound characteristically light, "don't tell me you're going to fire me, boss."

"Don't be an idiot, Vic. I'm worried about you. Are you all right?"

A silence, and labored breathing.

"Tell you the truth?"

"The truth," she answered, waving Bella out as she wandered in to see what was going on.

"Well, it seems that the rock caused a mild concussion which causes dizziness which causes me to fall flat on my ass every time I get out of bed. My physician, if you can call him that, tells me I have to stay in bed or a reasonable facsimile thereof for another day at least to give myself a chance to heal. Or something like that. I think it's stupid, but he charges too much for me to disobey him."

Dale picked up a pencil and began doodling on an invoice.

"Vic." She suddenly felt foolish, and afraid. She had to take a deep breath and speak rapidly before what courage she had fled. "Vic, do you feel up to some company tonight?"

"God, now she makes her move! You have lousy timing, lady, lousy timing."

Bella returned, this time refusing to obey Dale's angry gestures. She stood obstinately in the doorway, her arms folded across her chest.

"Vic, I'll be over tonight after we close. I'll bring some Chinese and we can talk, all right?"

"Talk? What kind of indecent proposal is that?"

"Later, Vic, I'm busy," and she hung up on his protests. "Bella, what is it?"

Bella's eyes squinted in disapproval. "There's an old woman out there who's giving me a hard time. She's after some chess set she says you had. I think it's the one I—"

Dale brushed her aside and moved along the back

of the store until she could look up the end aisle to the counter. She nodded and stepped back out of sight. It was Flora Campbell, still in black, bent over to examine the game boards. But her interest was patently feigned.

"Well?" Bella said behind her.

Dale grabbed at a shelf and spun around, swallowing a vicious response. She sighed instead. "That lady out there has been bothering me for months about the pieces you sold Dr. McPherson last summer. Remember them?"

Bella, intrigued, scratched at her neck before nodding.

"Good, then will you please do me a favor and get rid—"

"Miss Bartlett!"

Dale let loose a single curse that sent Bella back a step before brushing at her blouse while she composed her expression. Flora Campbell was waving from the counter, and Dale smiled, glared at Bella for not being a mind-reader and acting more quickly, and took her time heading up front. What, she thought, am I going to be thanked for this time—being there when her pet parrot died, for God's sake?

"Miss Bartlett," Flora said kindly, "I'm looking for something my poor David made not so long ago. Just before that terrible accident, in fact." She bent over again, studiously examining the two games still on display. "I don't see it here."

"If you mean the Children of Don," Dale said coldly, "I sold them only a couple of days after he brought them in."

Flora straightened quickly, her fingers like claws

on the edge of the counter. "How did you know they were the Children?" she demanded. "What do you know about them?"

"Only what Dave told me," she answered truthfully. "He named them for me when I asked."

"Did he say anything else?"

Dale mimed a show of trying to remember, extending it when she noticed the growing impatience that made the old woman fidget.

"No," she said at last, "not that I recall. He just pointed them out to me because I asked him to. For the customers, you understand, in case they wanted the information."

Flora drew herself up, her gaze imperious but lacking any inner authority. "Would you mind telling me who purchased the set, Miss Bartlett?"

"Would you mind telling me why you want to know, Miss Campbell?"

A visible debate deepened the wrinkles, then smoothed them to match her voice. "Why no, of course not. You see, poor Milly and I were going through some of his—Dave's—effects last night and we discovered the sketches for the pieces. Since he never told us about them and never sketched without making, I felt sure he had brought them here. I would like to know who has them because I'd like to try to buy them back."

"For sentimental reasons," Dale suggested.

"Exactly."

"They sold for quite a large sum, Miss Campbell. But not nearly as much as I might have gotten had I been the one who sold them."

"I realize that must be so, Miss Bartlett, but perhaps . . .'' and she shrugged while Dale smiled without mirth. ''Do you remember who it was who purchased them?''

''Sure I do. It was Ed McPherson.''

Flora hissed in a deep breath, swayed, and caught hold of the counter. Dale was too amazed to move to help her.

''McPherson,'' the old woman said, struggling for a smile. Then, almost to herself: ''I should have thought.''

''That's right,'' Dale said. ''He saw them through the window and nearly trampled a couple of girls. In fact, I was over there the other night and saw them displayed on his mantel. He's quite proud of them.''

''And he should be,'' Flora insisted. ''And he should be.'' She pressed a withered hand to her breast and nodded. ''Thank you, Miss Bartlett. I appreciate your help.''

Dale opened the door for her, stared after her as she moved slowly to the sidewalk. Her steps were forced, her balance unsteady, and Dale wondered if she should call a taxi, dismissed it and closed the door to cut off the afternoon chill. And when she turned, she almost bumped into Miss Inness who was standing directly behind her.

''Imagine that,'' Bella said, craning to follow the old woman's slow progress.

''Imagine what,'' Dale said.

''She was so angry at whatever you two were talking about, she forgot her accent.''

Dale nodded absently.

''And here.'' She pressed a slip of paper into

Dale's hand, then tapped it sharply when Dale didn't respond. "I thought you might still want it."

She looked down, opened her fingers.

"The note," Bella said. "I was straightening up your so-called office and found this thing in the bill file. Remember it? It was . . ." and she put two fingers to her temple in an attitude of concentration. A moment later she smiled. "Of course! It was the day poor Dave Campbell had his accident right out there in the street. Don't you remember, Dale? It was on the spindle when we came back. You were the one who found it, remember?"

Dale, reaching for a cardigan to drape over her shoulders, remembered.

# CHAPTER
# IX

On Devon Street, one block in from Mainland Road, was a brick-and-stone Georgian bastardization that had once belonged to Oxrun's only Washington representative. After his defeat at the start of the Depression, he sold the house to an enterprising family who knocked out walls, rearranged wiring, and affixed small balconies here and there to the second and third stories. The resulting apartment warren generally housed teachers, tellers, and the occasional instructor at the local junior college. Climbing, then, to Vic's second-floor-front quarters—two large rooms he'd divided into four with Chinese screens—Dale expected to find islands of dirty clothes begging for the laundry, a sink buried in dishes and frozen dinner trays, ashes ground into the unwaxed floor, and a thousand other horrors permanently attached to the bachelor living image.

But what she saw when Vic admitted her was a living room furnished in glass and chrome, and a wall-to-wall Oriental carpet in beige and royal blue; the kitchen alcove was spotless, the bedroom and bath clean enough for a nurse. Taken speechlessly aback, she spent the first few minutes prowling, craning at bookshelves that brushed the ceiling, admiring the oils he'd picked up in the city. Even the panes of the french doors were clean, she thought with a shake of her head; amazing.

"Disappointed, aren't you?" he said, guiding her to a corner of the thickly upholstered sofa. "You thought I'd be a slob and you could trot out your mothering instincts."

She shook her head numbly, and he laughed, poured her white wine from a crystal decanter and toasted her silently. Yet, in contrast to the room, he was wearing a worn plaid bathrobe over equally worn pajamas, and a pair of slippers she thought should have been discarded a decade before. He hadn't shaved in two days, and the shadow on his cheeks made his beard and mustache seem heavier and more unkempt. The head bandage was gone, only a small gauze patch remaining at his temple; and though she admitted that he looked better than he sounded, there was still a wan ghost at his face that suggested strain not yet shaken.

"Come on," he urged, "let me know what you think."

"I am impressed," she said slowly. "Man, but I'm impressed." She looked disdainfully at the cartons of Chinese food she'd carried with her, and stared at the ceiling. "Brother."

"Hey," he said, "let's not get ridiculous. I eat on paper plates, mostly. Who has time for dishes any more?"

Even after he'd fetched the paper plates and spooned out the meal, she doubted he had been telling the truth—but if that was what he wanted her to believe, then she would—for this night, at least.

They spoke little, eating slowly as if deliberately putting off the reason for her visit. But when the meal was done and the plates stashed in the garbage compactor, when the wine was poured in the soft light of a Tiffany lamp on the far corner, Vic lit a cigarette, leaned back and punched lightly at his stomach. "The first stuff I've been able to keep down all day. And now, Miss Bartlett, let's hear what you were babbling about this afternoon."

She opened her mouth, the prepared speech ready to fill the room and convince him of her fears. But it wouldn't come. It stuck, choked her, and she took a quick swallow of her wine. He kept silent when she pushed a nervous hand through her hair, said nothing when she slipped off her shoes and paced the length of the room to stop at the balcony doors and gaze out at the lights of the homes across the street.

"I thought I had it all down," she said finally, softly, without turning around. "So many things have been running through my head that I've given myself a dozen headaches." She told him of her visit to McPherson and the incident in the park the night before. She described the dream and its slow change, detailed her visit to the analyst's office and her abortive attempt to play the detective. "It was all so dumb, Vic. You should have seen me on the street today. People must have thought I was losing my mind, for God's sake.''

''You're not, you know. That's for sure.''

She moved from the doors and stood with the coffee table between them. Then she sank to the floor, crossing her legs and holding onto her ankles while she rocked rhythmically on her buttocks.

''I had even gone so far as to convince myself that Abe was right and the fire was only a freak accident. I almost did. But it wasn't.''

''I know.''

''You know it, and I know it, now. But for the life of me I couldn't be sure this afternoon, not until Bella handed me this.'' She reached into her blouse pocket and tossed him the note. He read it, eyebrows raised as he remembered, then folded it carefully and placed it on the table. ''It was like a click in my head,'' she said, struggling not to whisper. ''You know what I mean. It's so easy in the movies when the good guys can pull together a few simple facts and trot out their world-saving solutions. It's so easy, and so backward. Well . . .'' and she rubbed the back of her neck, ''maybe not that exactly, but close enough. The trouble was, see, I'd been taking all these things as isolated events. This and this belonged over here, and that and that belonged over there. No connections, no tie-ins, nothing like that.'' She frowned, ran the next words carefully through her mind while he watched, not staring, only waiting. ''You see, they are connected. All of them. And they started with that first note.''

Vic glanced at the paper, then looked up in surprise. "What? How did you come to that marvelous conclusion?"

"Well, pal, it was you who suggested the notes were written by some high school dopes who had a crush on me."

"Oh, it wasn't?"

"No," she said. "It wasn't. At least, not those kids." She reached out and jabbed at the paper. "This one was probably written by Jaimie. The other one was done by Willy Campbell."

Vic lighted another cigarette and puffed out a cloud they both followed to the ceiling.

"I don't have any real proof of this," she said, "but I think now this wasn't part of a love-note thing. I think . . . I think Willy wanted to tell me something, and he died before he could. I think this other one is a warning that had I gone to the park there would have been trouble. I don't know what this trouble is, or was, but look—Willy sends me the note, and dies; the second one comes, Dave gives me a strange chess set and, after McPherson nearly kills himself getting it out of the shop, Dave's car burns him up and we are nearly broiled in the orchard. And while all this is going on, you're getting fired, I'm getting dreams, and Ed goes on a stupid leave of absence for which there's no rational explanation." She rested her elbows on the table, shook a cigarette out of the pack and pointed it at him. "There's a lot of time between all this, nearly five months, but if you take away all those days when nothing went on . . . well, there's some kind of a connection.

"Somebody tried to murder us, Vic. We keep forgetting that, don't we? Like, maybe because we don't really want to believe it. But somebody tried to kill us."

He stared as an ember of tobacco fell onto the smoked glass. "And those visits from old—"

"Ridiculous!" she exclaimed. "I hardly know them at all. There was no feeling at all behind Flora and Milly coming to see me. Just like that time in the luncheonette, I get the feeling I'm being checked up on, that's all. I think . . . I think they're trying to see if I know something. Maybe something Willy told me. That conversation I heard last night? I think you and I are the 'other troubles' they were talking about."

"Okay, Dale, granting you that much, what are they doing that we're not supposed to know?"

She barked a laugh. "If I knew that, teach, I'd be camped in Abe's office right now. But listen, this is what really scares me." And as soon as she said it, she knew it was true. She was frightened—not for her life, but of whatever it was that was after it. "This afternoon Flora wanted to know if Dave said anything to me when he handed over the chess set. I told her he only explained what the pieces meant. It was a lie, Vic. He did say something else." She took a deep breath. "After Dave finished explaining everything, he said I should sell it to someone who was a traveler. Okay. Then, on the way out—and he was ready to cry, Vic!—he said . . . 'I wish I knew, fire or water.' "

She waited, her hands clenched, nails sparking into her palms. Vic crushed out the cigarette, rose, and walked a little unsteadily to the balcony doors. He opened them, and the night chill ghosted in. A car's horn, someone running, a slammed door and a young boy's whistle. He closed them, leaned against them.

"If I understand you, Dale, you're saying that what he said has something to do with the way he and his son died, and the way we were almost killed."

She let out a breath, sagged, and nodded gratefully. "I've thought about Dave's accident. Hitting that telephone pole shouldn't have set the car blazing like that, not ordinarily, not so soon. And Abe himself told me Willy shouldn't have drowned so fast. And . . . Elinor McPherson, drowned in the tub."

"My God, Dale," he said, dropping to his knees in front of her, "do you know what you're implying?"

She nodded again. "Willy was dead before the kids started their screaming. They, or someone else, murdered him."

"No! That can't be! I won't believe that, even if I swallow everything else. They're only kids, Dale. Kids, for crying out loud!"

"I will bet you," she said firmly, evenly, "that if you check with some of your friends on the grade-school faculty, you'll find the complaints about you did not originate with them. I'll bet you . . . I'll bet you my store to that ashtray that one or more of those kids deliberately kept mentioning your name when they showed off their new knowledge. Vic," she shouted, "they're doing something! I don't know what it is, but they are doing something."

Vic shifted until he was sitting back against the

coffee table, and she knew the incredulous feeling he was suffering while he tried to grasp what she'd already known to be true.

"Vic, the chessman I found in the field near your coat . . . again no proof, but I'm sure both Willy and Dave were holding something like it when they died."

His eyes narrowed, widened, and a hand played nervously at his mustache. She watched as he set up the facts and suppositions one at a time for his examination, and when he finally shook his head in reluctant, fearful admiration, she smiled. Broadly.

Because she was no longer alone.

"Five days," she said quickly. "That's what I heard last night, Vic. They're going to do something in five days."

"All right," he said. "Let's see . . . five days is what, Halloween? Thursday? What's that supposed to mean? Ghosts and goblins and a few Campbell witches?"

"No, that's not right. It's not Halloween, Vic, it's the first of November. It's Friday. This Friday."

Vic started to nod, then shook his head. "Now wait a minute. That's All Saints' Day, and there's nothing sinister about that that I can think of. Maybe what we ought to do is get hold of Abe or Fred and let them know what we've got. I mean, we've got some admittedly wild accusations here, but they do seem to hold together."

"Don't be stupid," she said. "They only hold together because we've made them do it. What do they call it . . . circumstantial evidence? You couldn't convict Jack the Ripper with what we have."

"Okay, boss, so what do we do, then?"

She stared at him. "Do? That's what you're supposed to figure out. I'm too tired to think any more."

"Maybe they're midget revolutionaries. Kidnap the village and hold all us millionaires for ransom."

"Vic, will you please be serious?"

"Well how can I be? I mean, really, Dale . . . all we—"

"The library," she said, snapping her fingers. "Maybe we can find out about the date in the library."

"Great," he said with little enthusiasm. "And after we pick up something—assuming there's anything to pick up—we'll march right over to Ed's and tell him his kid is trying to bump us off because he's having a kindergarten witches' sabbath in a few days and we know it and he thinks we'll try to stop it. Dale, do you know what he'll say?"

"I can imagine," she said sourly.

"So can I."

"But what about the chessmen?"

"What about them?"

"If Flora was so upset about not finding them, they must have some significance in this thing. Maybe it'll give us something more substantial to work with. Anything," she added, "will be better than just sitting around shouting at each other."

Bless you, Natalie Clayton, Dale thought as they stepped into the warmth of the library's late hours. The main floor was a spacious two stories high and lighted by great white cylinders that held back the night from the gray glass wall that fronted the building. She and Vic stood hesitantly by the door, rubbing hands and arms until the cold vanished, scanning the vast room carefully. The children's section on the right was colorful and deserted, the new fiction and magazines area on the left held a few college-age browsers. At the horseshoe counter in the center that divided the reading sections from the stacks was a middle-aged woman struggling with a series of computer print-outs apparently reluctant to separate from the attached sheets of carbon.

"Where?" Vic whispered.

Dale shrugged, then pulled him toward the card catalogue. "Dave called them the Children of Don and the Children of Llyr. That must have something to do with it." She pulled out several file drawers and, with a nudge to his ribs, began flicking through the cards. She let her cold-numbed fingers move slowly to allow her more time to think of what she was doing. Once she'd passed some of her fear to Vic she felt as if she was becoming more and more a part of some vast production in which time was meaningless, the moves she made and the speeches she uttered less of her own volition than devices leading her somewhere on a stage considerably more vast than the village she lived in—an uneasy sense of manipulation she could not shake off.

Either that, or she was becoming a mindless hysteric.

"Nothing," Vic muttered, slamming a drawer back into place. "This isn't going to get us anywhere at all."

"Sure it will," she insisted, grabbing at his sleeve when he turned away. "Come on, Vic, we can't drop

it now. Let me think a minute." Dave, the chessmen, the names . . . the names . . . "Wait a minute!
He said something about their being from his Highland background. That's not the way he put it exactly, but maybe we can look up something there."

"You're nuts," he said. "Highland isn't going to
get us anything but travel books and pretty pictures.
What we need are some mythology books." He
snapped his fingers. "Sure! Celtic mythology."

Success had them in and out of the stacks in less
than five minutes. They took one of the circular
tables scattered between the counter and the entrance,
and spread the half-dozen volumes in front of them.

"First one with the goods wins a prize," Vic said.

"Which is?"

"Me."

She sat back in the wooden chair and folded her
arms. "I'm not playing."

"Suit yourself, lady. I'm the best there is."

She watched him as he bent over a large open
book. His hair, blown askance by the wind, fell over
his face, veiling it. His hands moved swiftly through
the pages, stopping to point, tapping in a margin as
he read. Victor, she thought suddenly, why do I feel
so damned protective of you? God knows you're a
grown man. He glanced up once, frowned mock-
ingly, returned to grab another book and set it atop
the one already before him. And despite the others
milling about the floor, the woman slapping paper
down on the counter, they were alone. Warm, and
alone. As they were in the store, signaling to each
other across the aisles, anticipating complaints, com-

ments, customer needs. No wonder Bella often felt as though she was a third wheel—Vic's coming had created an axis from which the older woman had been excluded, spinning in her own orbit with only the toys and the people for anchors.

She blinked.

"Vic, I love you."

He looked up again, grinned, and suddenly looked away.

This is insane, she told herself; this is incredibly insane. I'm supposed to be frightened out of my wits. I'm supposed to be hunting for a clue to something that could blot me out like some minor error in my ledgers; and I'm so idiotically happy I feel like tearing off my clothes they're so tight, screaming and shouting and playing the fool! It's insane!

The puzzle faded, then, and in its place a desire to grab Vic and get out, run to her house and pack and take his car as far as they could drive. What happened in Oxrun Station could be forgotten, whatever danger there was passed and over. An episode, nothing more, to be laughed at as they walked along some distant beach jeering at their imaginations until memory eroded the nightmare.

"Vic."

"Here," he said, and slapped at a page. "For what it's worth, I've found it."

"Vic, I don't want to—"

He picked up the book, turned it round so she could see the illustrations. They were sketches based on artifacts, remnants of a British Olympiad before the coming of Caesar and his Romans.

Her protests evaporated.

As she pulled the volume toward her, he leaned forward until their heads were almost touching. "According to this, there were essentially two groups of gods: the Children of Don, and the Children of Llyr. It's hard to keep later Christian influence separate from the originals, but apparently these two weren't in any state of rival hostilities. They just co-existed depending upon the beliefs of the inhabitants. Probably a lot of them were borrowed from the Irish."

It took little effort for Dale to see in the faces before her the carvings Dave had made, that McPherson now owned.

"Like all kinds of religions, these folk had their feast days and holy days and good stuff like that." His whisper was close to her ear, and she shuddered. "These people, for instance, have things called Imbolc, Lugnasad, and Beltine. Fertility and all that because the Celts were agricultural folk, it seems. They also have the Feast of Samain. The first of November."

Dale listened as Vic's voice became hypnotic in its eagerness, and he flipped the pages quickly to show her the pre-Roman representations of the gods, the dolmen where the dead were buried, the demigods who were the warrior heroes. And the feast of Samain where the old and new years met and Time belonged to neither, when the harvests were in, the flocks and hunts completed. It wasn't difficult for her to understand the Celtic fear of winter when the land died and the skies grayed and the cold air from the North brought sickness and privation. She glanced up at the light directly overhead, then to the dim glow of the street lamps. No, not difficult to understand at all.

A shadow paused at the entrance. The door opened slightly, closed quickly, and she rubbed at her eyes. Tired, she thought; I would have sworn that was Liz.

"Now," Vic said, sweeping the books to one side and taking her hands, "are you listening, kid? The thing of it is, on this feast day or whatever it was, those who believed in the gods and goddesses and all those spooky things also believed that men, ordinary men, could walk into the Otherworld through what I guess you could call sacred mounds—*side* is the name for them—and the opposite happens, too. What happens then, I don't know. Probably, depending on where you lived as a card-carrying Celt, you either had good times living it up with a gorgeous immortal vamp, or the gods who weren't all that lovely did ungood things to you.

"The question is, of course, now that we know all about this—so what? You're surely not going to tell me we've got some dyed-in-the-wool Celtic believers right here in little old Oxrun Station. You try it, and I'll flatten that gorgeous nose of yours."

"You didn't tell me about the sacrifices."

He couldn't hide the guilt that shadowed his face.

"Come on, Vic, I can read, too. I saw that part about the fire and water."

Suspicion based upon folk tales and fragments of mythology, rites gleaned from Druidic colleges where knowledge was passed down by rote. Hints and conjectures that Samain included human and animal sacrifices—a man, a woman, a child slaughtered, entrails and limbs burned and ashes scattered; a man, a woman, a child forced into a lake or stream and held down until drowned. All in propitiation for the coming new year.

"Now," she said, "tell me what I'm trying to make you believe."

"No. I can't do that. I can't because I think it's absurd. In the first place—in the main place—we live where there hasn't been an immigration wave since the day the Pilgrims set up shop on the coast. Aside from those families who have sneaked in here and there, the line of Oxrun blood goes back uninterrupted for a couple of hundred years. Your family goes back to the Revolution, for crying out loud. Nobody here would know what a Celt or a Samain was if they fell over them."

"Nobody but the Campbells."

"The Campbells are Scots."

"So they say. But Flora does keep losing that accent, doesn't she? And what we're talking about is basically Welsh, isn't it?"

His mouth opened, shut, and he rubbed at his jaw while avoiding her stare.

"Okay, Dale, I'll grant you something more. That the Campbells aren't Scots, and it's just possible the old lady and her crew still hold to the ways of her ancestors. That really isn't so far-fetched considering the dolts who still believe in witchcraft and Satanism and things like that. Maybe they even still worship some of the gods and consider the fast days part of their beliefs. But so what? It's not a crime, you know."

"No, but murder—attempted and otherwise—sure is."

"Dale, I'll say it again, slowly, so you'll understand. We have no proof. And if you think I'm going to tell Abe Stockton that we think there are a bunch of crazy Celts running around Oxrun Station getting ready to sacrifice our good citizens, if you think I am going to face him with that, then you're just as crazy as they are."

But Willy was too soon dead; Dave's car blazing to furnace; and the orchard flaring to hellfire.

She saw the confusion in his face and sympathized; it was the identical turmoil she'd weathered that afternoon—the modern mind trained to deal with phenomena logically and demanding reason uncover the solution for the seemingly inexplicable; the modern mind taught to discard the fantasies, the tales, the Scots' bumps in the night. Reason. Logic. So simply stated, so fearfully held onto. Reason and Logic, the modern gods in a godless world.

"Let's walk," Vic said. "I need some air."

She held his arm tightly, as much for comfort as to hold him up. Though he said nothing, she knew his dizziness was returning and she wanted to scold him for coming out even though it was her doing. But when she tried to bring it up, he hushed her angrily, refusing to admit to or succumb to the weakness.

Hypothesis, she thought: the Campbells, for whatever reason, have somehow clung to or revived portions of a prehistoric Celtic religion, carried this belief to their new home in Oxrun and, probably through the childtalk of Willy and the solemn honesty of Dave, brought others into their circle. It was, however, easier to believe how the children, with talk of demons and gods and otherworldly excitement, could be infected with temporary enthusiasm; but it wasn't so easy to see how Ed, with all his medical and psychological training, could be affected too. And as far as she knew, he was the only adult outside the family who subscribed to this nonsense.

Question, she thought: why three deaths? The Campbells couldn't realistically expect persecution for their unusual religion—at the most, derision and scorn, and that could be escaped easily by moving to another small community, or a larger one in which to be lost.

The early evening's chill turned to a damp cold. The thick-limbed trees and smattering of fir fragmented the waterfall glow of the street lights. They were alone, and it was silent, no hints at all of radios or televisions or even a domestic quarrel seeping through the dark walls of the homes they passed. Deliberately, Dale walked lightly, not wanting to disturb the peace that moved with them. It was sufficient that they were together, isolated, wondering silently if what they had learned in the library was applicable or wasted.

Vic stumbled, and she held him tighter, pressing her cheeck to his arm while a hand stole about her waist and squeezed.

"All right," he said finally. "There's no way around it. We'll toss a coin and face one of them."

She blinked away her scattered thoughts and asked what he meant.

"Easy. We'll go . . . we'll go to see Ed and tell him what we think. That he's part of some cult and we're worried that someone inside thinks we're out to harm it. We'll assure him we're not, promise to stay away, and hope that they—whoever they are—will leave us alone.''

''What if he doesn't know anything about it?''

''We'll tell him anyway. He must know Jaimie's a part of it. And if that's incorrect, he'll know about it when we're done. Either way we'll have done all we can. It's as simple as that.''

Not so simple, she thought, and said so. ''Besides, suppose he refuses to leave us alone. Assuming your assumptions are right.''

''Then we'll go talk to Fred and tell him everything we think, everything we suspect. Abe was right about one thing, you know—this itch of his needs to be scratched, and I doubt that he's satisfied even now. This will at least give him something to think about.''

''Or laugh at.''

''Or laugh at. Look, Dale, either we do this or we work ourselves into one magnificent panic that's going to send the both of us to the loony bin within a week.''

''We could forget about it.''

He laughed, a slow and easy laugh that barely ruffled the quiet of the street. ''Easier said than done, to coin an old cliché. No, we aren't able to do something like that. I vote we visit Ed tomorrow or the next day and do as I said. The worst he can do is throw us out of his house and order us never to darken his door again. Right?''

''Right,'' she said. ''Right.''

But it was wrong. All wrong. The worst he could do . . .

Without speaking, then, they returned to the apartment and sat on the floor cradling cups of warm cider. She didn't know when it happened, but sometime before midnight she was in his arms, crying first, and then sighing.

He promised her the moon.

She promised to star it.

He told her he was afraid.

She loved him for it.

And he fell asleep while she held him, on the floor, in the moonlight. She kissed his brow, and stretched out beside him, and slept, dreamless. But not at all well.

# CHAPTER
# X

Tuesday's sky lost its blue. At midmorning a straggle of clouds thinned to form a dull haze beneath the sun, like drifting smoke from a distant forest fire. By noon a light breeze stole into Centre Street, plucking at sweaters and skirts timidly, nudging dead leaves along the trails of the gutters until they were caught at the storm drains, fluttering helplessly. Gems set on black velvet trays lost their natural radiance, mannequins yielded their pretense to humanity, and the fluorescent lighting of the luncheonette took on an unnatural and unflattering harsh glare.

It was, as Bella said, a soulless day, when not even a quilted bedspread would be comfort enough.

Dale agreed, but for different reasons. Vic's doctor had visited him that morning and had ordered him back to bed for at least two more days. Vic tried to tell her how brave he had been, fending off the doctor's authority with manly protests and displays of inner courage; but she knew he was exhausted still, and told him with a laugh he'd better get into shape before he tried to handle her again.

"Woman," he said, "the day I can't handle you is the day I turn in my macho badge."

"Sleep," she ordered before she rang off. "I'll call you tonight when I get home."

"What home?"

"My home," she answered. "You're in no condition for a wrestling match with an Amazon."

He'd laughed, then, and was still chuckling when she hung up and propped her chin forlornly in a palm. The day was going to drag, she thought, what with the weather and Vic; and it did. Few customers and fewer sales left her with nothing to do but tackle invoices and preorders for the Christmas season. Halloween was only two days away and most of her gadget and costume supplies were already depleted—the one advantage of being a specialty shop in a town without a shopping mall.

She considered visiting McPherson by herself, thought about it less than a minute before deciding she was too much of a coward to go without Vic.

Lord, this is terrible, she thought—but home was worse. The house was damp, springing drafts where she swore there had been none the year before. Immediately after eating, she wandered, turning on all the lights, spending an hour with her plants in the fancied dream that one of them would miraculously break through an evolutionary barrier and gain the power of speech. The television helped, but not much;

the voices of the actors, the newsmen, the commercial families were tinny and unreal, forced and stilted, as if they knew what she wanted and couldn't bring themselves to help.

And for the first time in months she took a sleeping pill, then another to be sure she wouldn't find shadows where there were no lights.

Wednesday, then, should have been an improvement, the day before Vic's return. But, though anticipation made the morning hours agony, a call when she returned from lunch turned the afternoon to hell.

"What do you mean, another day?" She gripped the receiver tightly, feeling perspiration clinging slickly to her hand. "What's he doing to you?"

"All sorts of evil and diabolical experiments," Vic said, unable to disguise his disappointment. "But he said I'm not eating well enough to recover fast enough. Dear Emma has been dragooned into fixing me hearty meals for the duration."

"I'll bring something over to cook."

"No, you won't," he said. "I'm sorry, Dale love, but if you come over here, I'll be set back a thousand years. Besides, when your doctor also happens to be your landlady's husband, and they engage in a vile conspiracy to make you get better, you'd best not fool around."

Her voice was little-girl small. "Can I call you later?"

"If you don't, kid, I'll rape dear Emma and spend the rest of my days drawing obscene pictures on my cell wall."

After hanging up, an image: pale, pouches of dark under his eyes, cheeks hinting at hollows, and the slight trembling of his left hand. She gnawed on her lips and lit a cigarette.

"You're smoking too much," Bella admonished. "He's not going to die, you know."

She knew that, but she couldn't quite shake the feeling that unless he was with her she would fall apart like a puzzle in an earthquake. And on the face of it, it was ridiculous. She'd been too independent to suddenly surrender her individuality to the strength of one man; yet she was unable to shed the sense of loss, and she kept sneaking glances at the door, the aisles, the storeroom in back, hoping he'd suddenly pop up with his huge grin flaring the ends of his mustache while his hands waggled a private semaphore warning her old lady Mardon was rearranging the doll houses again.

Just before closing, she interrupted Bella's leaving and plucked nervously at nonexistent lint. "Bella, how did you feel when you first met your husband?"

Bella folded her wrinkles into an attitude of concentration, crossed her arms over her ample breasts and stared at the ceiling. Dale felt, then, she was being mocked until a short, abrupt smile changed her mind.

"I hated him," she said. "I thought he was the most boorish, crude, and foul-mouthed gutter creature that I'd ever been forced into company with. He was my father's idea, so he claimed, and that first blind date was an absolute horror." She shifted her hands to pat at her hips. "I was plump even then, believe it or not, and he kidded me about it the entire evening. He saw me twice more after that before the

Army took him against the Kaiser.'' A third time, and her hands clasped at her waist. Clenched until her knuckles were bloodless. "When he was gone— three years and three months—I knew what it felt like to be a Siamese twin without the twin.'' Then she smiled, the most warming smile Dale had ever seen her admit to. "Dear, if you count the hours, he'll never get back.''

Dale only nodded. And when she was alone, the store dark and the windows leering their skeleton masks and witches' caldrons, she let her lips part in a foolish, sheepish grin. It stayed, and she didn't care, while Celts and gods and flaming arrows vanished until a dark figure appeared at the door, pounding furiously on the glass. She uttered a short scream before the shouted words penetrated and she flung open the door to let Vic storm in, grabbing her, hugging her, then flicking on the lights and boosting himself to sit on the counter.

"I give up,'' she said, not knowing whether to be angry or to give way to the joy that threatened to explode her. "What are you doing out of bed?''

He unbuttoned his coat, flung it behind him like a cape. "Listen, I got to thinking about raping dear Emma, which naturally led to filthy thoughts about you, which . . .'' and his face darkened, "which led me to the unpleasant reminder that we have only two days before Friday. I can't let this,'' and he slapped at his head, "get in the way.''

"But, Vic—''

"But Vic nothing. I can always collapse on Satur- day if I have to. Right now I have too much to do.''

"Like what?'' she asked.

He blew out a breath, stretched his neck, rubbed at his chest. Then, nodding, he eased off his perch and handed over her coat.

"Like what?" she asked again, balking when he opened the door and pushed her outside, stopping only long enough to set the alarms and the lock. "Come on, Vic, let's not play games, all right?"

"No games," he agreed. "First we eat. Then we pay a visit to our local analyst and apparently spooky scholar. After that, well, we'll play it by ear. What do we have to lose?"

"Don't ask such stupid questions."

They sat in the upper room of the Chancellor Inn, a randomly intimate arrangement of two-person booths done in soft brown leather. A ceiling-high fireplace dominated the room, and thick oaken doors blocked out the noise from the dining/dancing areas on the first floor. They spoke little save to order duck and wine, and when the meal arrived they avoided each other's glances as if suddenly embarrassed to be found together in public. Dale knew it was a fine repast, but the taste of the fowl was lost as she struggled not to dwell on what she had known had been coming for the past two days. It was no longer a matter of being made a fool of—she would have given all that she had to insure that outcome—but what concerned her now was an incident which had occurred that afternoon; and as she told Vic about it, her wine turned sour.

"They came in," she said, "looking for a chemistry set for a younger cousin. At least, that's what they told Bella. Now I can tell you right now that the

Newcastles' nearest relatives are somewhere down in Jersey; and this sudden love for an absent cousin was garbage from the word go. What happened was, the twins cornered Mrs. Inness near where the sets were and made her open every one of them. They said they were checking them out in case a piece or two was missing.''

"Like all else," Vic said, "it has the impeccable face of innocence. Young kids learning good consumerism from their parents, and all that."

"Right, I agree. But they didn't buy anything. Nothing was missing. They just didn't buy anything! What they did do was pester the poor woman with a million questions. You know—what does this do, why does this happen when you mix this thing with that thing, how is a magnet made—things Bella wouldn't know even if she was still going to school!"

"Curiosity," he said, the devil's advocate.

"Sure. And when Bella told them to check the library if they were so interested, Carol, I think it was, told her Mrs. Clayton would only let them use the young people's encyclopedia. They already knew what that one said, Carol told Bella, and it wasn't sufficient."

"Sufficient for what? A damned bomb?"

Dale shook her head. "I honestly don't know. But it left the poor woman pretty shaken up. They weren't just being curious, you know. They were actually demanding answers. Demanding, Vic! And it isn't the first time. You've had to go through this and so have I. A million times over the past few months, but never as bad as this."

He gazed blankly over her shoulder and scraped a

fork over his plate. "Yeah. Yeah, they have. Not the twins for me, but Carl has, and Melody. Jaimie, once, when I first started working there. Pumping me just as though . . ." He set his fork on the table and shoved back his chair. "Come on," he said. "We can grab something else later if you're still hungry. We don't have time to finish up here."

Dale didn't argue. She smiled apologetically at the maître d' and murmured nonsense disclaimers to the waiter who hovered after them as they hurried to the cloakroom. She knew what Vic was going to say: it was just like the sessions he had had with the same kids when they visited the high school yard. Only now she knew it wasn't the company of the older kids that they were after. It was the picking of brains, both student and teacher. Bella had once called them an unruly gang of precocious brats; but they weren't precocious, not in the ordinary sense of the word. It was as though they had been shipwrecked for half a century on some desert island and were trying to find out what had happened to the world since they had been gone.

Not precocious.

Hungry.

"Assuming you're thinking the same thing I'm thinking," he said as they descended to the front door and the parking lot, "what do you think?"

"Assuming that makes sense," she answered with a half-grin, "I don't know. Another piece to consider for the time being, that's all."

Traffic was still considerably heavy, and it was some time before Vic was able to cross the Pike and pull into McPherson's block. The headlights glittered off the hurricane fence, and the cemetery beyond was a wall of impenetrable black. A huge white Persian cat raced down the sidewalk after a small dark shadow Dale hoped wasn't a chipmunk; and as they moved up the flagstone walk toward the house she wondered why anyone would let so valuable a cat loose anyway—something as beautiful as that she would have turned into a house pet, not an alley cat with a pedigree.

"Witch's familiar," Vic muttered, reading her thought, and she slapped him on the back, hard, but grateful he'd broken the tension that had transformed her spine into a lead rod that kept her head high, her shoulders uncomfortably straight.

"So ring," she said when they reached the stoop. "He can't see through the walls, you know."

And when he did, quickly, barely touching the glowing plastic button, she heard the grandfather clock chiming. "Eight o'clock, and all's well," she said under her breath.

"What do you know that I don't," he said, then broke into a hearty smile when the door opened and Ed gaped out at them. "Hey, you going to let us freeze out here? Winter's coming, Ed."

McPherson recovered, but not before Dale noticed him flick the hand at his side and heard a scurrying in the front room.

Immediately they went in and were seated, still coated, on the couch, Ed handed them thin glasses of sherry and began a litany of probing Vic's health, expressing concern over his loss of weight and appealing to Dale to take better care of him. It ran on interminably, and she wanted to scream at him to halt the flow of oral garbage. But in his striped shirt and maroon sweater-vest, sharply creased black slacks and highly polished shoes, he was the stereotype of urbanity, the ultra-casual small-town font of psychological wisdom. He would not be stopped, and she didn't try to interrupt when she saw Vic playing his game solemnly, as though he actually cared what McPherson felt and was going out of his way to smother him in reassurances.

Finally, Ed lost his momentum. He rose from the armchair and stood next to the fireplace while Dale prayed he wouldn't lift his arm to prop the elbow on the mantel. And when he did, she closed her eyes briefly and sighed.

"But now," McPherson said, knocking his pipe against the brass globe of an andiron, "it's your turn to monopolize, my friends. It looks as if this unexpected dropping in is getting to be a habit." He grinned at Dale, who returned it painfully.

"Well, Ed," Vic began, shifting to drape an arm over the back of the sofa, "Dale and I here have ourselves a small problem, and we hope you can help us see the light."

Ed's laugh was girlish, too nervous to be genuine. "Seems to me you'd want to see a preacher, there, Victor."

"Well, maybe it will come to that," Vic said, "but I doubt it. You see, Ed, a couple of things have happened over the past few months—four or five, actually—that makes us think that your son is getting himself into trouble he won't be able to handle."

Ed instantly glanced at the chessboard on the mantel. Dale saw his lips moving, counting. "I don't really follow you, Vic,'' he said. ''I didn't think you were connected with the school system any more.''

Vic admitted as much. ''The thing is, Jaimie used to be a good friend of Willy Campbell. You remember him. The boy who was—''

''Drowned in the pond. I remember it well. A tragic affair, wasn't it, Dale?''

Startled to be so suddenly included, she could only nod mutely.

''Indeed,'' Vic said, drawing McPherson's attention back to himself. ''Well, it seems that the Campbells are a little old-fashioned in their religious beliefs. To put it mildly. I suppose you could say they've resurrected some of their ancestors' rather bizarre tenets and their emphasis on Olympus-type gods and magic and things like that. Apparently it's fascinated some of the local children. Jaimie among them.''

''No!'' Ed snapped. ''Not at all. My son is too level-headed for nonsense like that. His personality is extremely well adjusted for a boy his age.'' He paced away from the hearth, glanced down the hall, and returned to his chair. ''He doesn't believe in anything like that. Nothing.''

''Well, I for one don't know about that,'' Dale said. The sternness she faced was a façade, nothing more, and it was his eyes that gave McPherson away, betrayed the fragile control he was exerting on his nerves. ''I mean, he's always in the store picking up the latest monster model or the mechanical sets he builds those robots and creatures with. Only the other day he—''

''Boy's play,'' Ed said. ''He doesn't believe it,

but that doesn't mean he can't pretend that he does. Why, he has never even believed in Santa Claus, as far as I can remember. His mother, she used to fret about that all the time, but . . ." He swallowed hard, making sure they noticed the action of his throat. Then he drew himself up and allowed an indignant glare to settle over his features. "And what, may I ask, is there about this so-called fascination of my son's which makes it any of your business?"

"Oh come on, Ed, get off it," Vic said. "We're friends, remember?"

"Friends do not pry," he said primly. "They—"

"We are not prying!" Vic exploded, pounding a fist on the end table and causing the lamp to sway. "We said we thought there was a potential problem for you, and we presumed our friendship was strong enough that we could come to you and let you know."

"Victor, please! Your voice!" Ed cautioned softly. "The boy's in his room."

Dale wanted to deride the show of protection, coughed instead and crossed her legs. "Ed"—and he snapped his head in her direction, making her think he was feeling under siege, beset by enemies on either flank—"Ed, we thought you weren't really feeling very well. We didn't want—"

"What are you talking about, not feeling well? What the hell are you doing, checking up on my medical history, too?"

"No," she said calmly, refusing to raise her voice to match his own, "I wanted to see you the other day about a change that happened with my dreams— remember them?—and the receptionist in your office told me you had let your regular secretary go and were on a long leave of absence.''

"Oh, that. Well, she got it wrong, as usual. Miss Evans is on a trip to see a sick relative. And I am only taking a couple of weeks of well-earned vacation. I mean, even a doctor has the right to a vacation, doesn't he?'' He tapped his pipe against his teeth. "I haven't been off in several years—five, I think it is—and Jaimie convinced me I should take it easy for a while. Loaf around and get to know him better. It's hard, you know, being both mother and father to a boy. When school's in, that's one thing, but when the summer comes around he needs someone around the house to talk to when he needs it. There's nothing wrong with that, is there?''

The last was nearly a plea. His composure had slipped, and Dale realized with an almost tangible shock that he wanted them out of the house, that he was afraid of something and he didn't want them around.

Vic had picked up the slip at the same time, and when he rose to leave, she voiced no objection. They walked slowly to the door, heard Ed moving behind them before he came up and slapped Vic's side in false comradeship.

"I'm a little tired," he said weakly.

"It's all right, Ed," Vic said, opening the door. "I'm sorry if we disturbed you."

"You didn't disturb me," he said, suddenly brusque again. "I'm just glad to be able to put your minds at rest. Jaimie," he said eagerly, "is a good boy. He won't get into trouble. Don't you worry about him. He won't get into any trouble."

The door fairly slammed in their faces and, though Dale wanted to stand by the window, Vic pulled her roughly off the stoop and to the car. Without a word he started the engine and sped down to the Pike, turned the corner and slammed the car to a halt at the curb. When she glared at him, he grinned.

"You wanted to snoop, didn't you, kid? Well, what are we waiting for?"

# CHAPTER
# XI

What Dale wanted was a miracle. A huge god-hand reaching out of the dark to pluck car and Vic and her out of Oxrun Station, set them down in another country, on another planet; it made no difference just as long as they were away from what she feared she would discover if she surrendered to Vic's urgings. It was, she thought with a cast back to her college classics, her own personal Rubicon—and the waters were raging, struggling to drag her down into a cold black nothing where terror took the place of death, and death was an escape to heaven.

"Dale," Vic said, poking her arm, "are you all right?"

I don't want to be a martyr.

"Hey, Dale!"

I don't want to die. I don't want to know.

"Dale, damnit!"

She started, realizing she hadn't been speaking aloud. She turned to tell him to start the car and drive away, saw the look on his face and knew that the river had already been crossed.

"Girding my loins," she said, hoping the darkness in the car would hide the weakness of her grin.

"Gird away, kid," he said quietly, "but don't strangle yourself. We either go now or we don't go at all."

The door handle was cold. She wished she had brought a pair of gloves. A quick whistle, then, to summon courage from wherever it was hiding, and she was out onto the grass, the sidewalk, waiting for a passing truck to let Vic join her.

They moved at a slow trot back up the street, keeping on the edges of the neighbors' lawns to smother their footsteps. Twice Dale caught herself holding her breath as if that one small addition to the noise they were making would be the spring that crashed the trap down around them. The overcast breeze had not let up; and with the stars now gone, the cold seemed deeper as it stung her nostrils, lips, and lungs. A fine preparation for Halloween, she thought as they angled farther onto the grass toward the side of McPherson's house, but definitely not right for prowling in the middle of the night. Her ears became numb and, as she reached up a hand to rub at them, she stumbled over something hidden in the lawn. A muttered curse as Vic grabbed at her shoulders. The breeze gusted briefly into a wind and her eyes watered. Her sleeve was sandpaper as it brushed them clear, and she winced at the stinging the gesture produced.

There was a neatly trimmed border of waist-high juniper pressed close to the house, and as they moved cautiously into it, the rustling was magnified by the fear that they would be caught by Ed with no reasonable explanation, or means of escape. Dale waited at the front corner, then, while Vic checked the front room. And as she watched him crouched in front of the window off the stoop, the Persian returned to sit boldly on the lawn and stare at her. She flicked an impatient hand, tried a nervously soft hiss before reaching down and tossing a pebble at it. It didn't move, only licked at one paw until, fearful that Ed would look at her and wonder what had intrigued the animal so, she took an angry step toward it. A pebble, a hiss, and another step, and it arched its back, stretched its front legs slowly, and wandered off across the street. When Dale looked down at her hand, she saw it was trembling violently and she crushed it against her side, willing it to be calm and too afraid to see if she had succeeded.

Suddenly there was a loud thudding crash from inside the house, just behind her head. She spun around as Vic rejoined her. A single window, heavily curtained, cast a rectangle of dim white onto the frost-stiffened grass. The sound of the crash settled behind it, and there were muffled voices in its place. Vic motioned for her to move up to the glass, but she shook her head. He became adamant, shoved her forward through the narrow gap between shrub and wall and she had to grab at the slightly protruding sill to keep from losing her balance. The voices were louder now, and with a hurried warning to Vic to keep a close eye on the curtains, she pressed her ear against the pane. She jumped at another smashing from within. There was no doubt Ed and Jaimie were arguing about something; their voices shifted around the room, fading and clearing as though they were shouting into a strong variable wind.

". . . rid of them, didn't I? What more do you want? They won't be . . . my word for it. Now for . . . leave me be!"

"They could not have known unless . . . wrong about Willy . . . you, wasn't it? It was, it had to be . . . thought you wanted to help us and . . . not keep our promise."

Something wooden slammed against the wall, and there was a man's yell, desperate and frightened.

A silence.

Then, Jaimie once again, this time in a language Dale could not understand—a guttural sound of almost Teutonic harshness that made her wonder if the window and the wind had combined to garble what she heard.

"Speak English!" Ed snapped suddenly. "You can't get around if you're going to jabber!"

A murmuring followed. Dale grimaced as she tried to force meaning into the sounds, with the glass a numbing cold against her head. Then, at a warning from Vic, she ducked. Jaimie was standing directly in front of the window, his shadow visible and wavering against the curtain.

"We will speak of it later. It is a shaméd thing, is it not? Elinor, Will, and David. And now it seems it is you, Edwin. I do not know yet. I will know in some time. But it be a full shaméd thing. I will have to take a walk now. Do not go where I be, Edwin. We have not many time left.''

The shadow moved, shrank, and Dale pushed away from the wall. She grabbed at Vic's sleeve and pushed him through the juniper, ran with him through the border of poplar that separated the McPhersons from their immediate neighbors. There was no time for questions. At any instant she expected to hear a door slam, followed by an angry shout of discovery. But they reached the car safely, and Vic was pulling away from the curb before she could close her door.

She held up her hands, their coldred skin purple in the light of the dash. But they were steady, and she didn't know how that could be. By the feeling in her stomach, they should have shaken themselves off their wrists before she knew what was happening.

"God," Vic said. "Okay, so now where?"

She waved the question away, not trusting herself to speak. A glance at her watch, and it was nearly fifteen minutes to nine. Almost an hour since they first arrived at McPherson's. A little more than three hours and it would be Halloween. Something like twenty-seven hours and it would be the first of November. And . . . she stopped herself, knowing that one more count would set her to laughing, a laughing she wouldn't be able to stop.

Vic turned onto Mainland Road and headed slowly north. They passed the village, the cemetery, moved into the thick woodlands that flanked the road and climbed the low hills that blocked out the sky. Oncoming traffic glared its headlights, vanished, appeared, like waves of blaring white. A huge buck and its doe and fawn froze on the graveled shoulder, eyes gleaming redly; Dale turned when they passed, saw the animals move single file over the highway and leap darkly into the brush on the opposite side. A two-pump gas station cowered under its bright lights, a man in its small office seated in front of a portable television. Then, a side road without an identifying signpost, and Vic suddenly wrenched the wheel, spinning them over gravel until the automobile straightened and they were alone.

They were on a narrow one-lane road more dirt than macadam. Denuded branches clutched into an open tunnel above them. And there was only the quiet mutter of the engine and the crunch of studded tires until Dale blinked herself out of the thoughts threatening to make her scream. She shifted to sit partially against the door, shivering at the cold seeping in through the window, and cleared her throat.

"That . . . that wasn't his voice."

"I heard."

"My God, Vic, that wasn't his voice!"

It was entirely possible, she told herself, that what she heard had been a trick of the windows, the walls, the muffling of the heavy curtains—but Jaimie's voice had, at the last, become somberly deep, a pounding piano bass that pronounced rather than conversed, commanded rather than proposed. And the whining belonged to Ed McPherson, psychologist and father—a simpering, slithering squeal piping from a man in fear of his life.

"I do not believe in things like satanic possession."

"Neither do I, Dale, neither do I."

"Then what did we hear?"

No answer. She knew there couldn't be one, not one that made any sense.

The car slowed gradually as the road began to twist, turning back upon itself, narrowing, gaping great holes that seldom were repaired. Ruts that jerked the wheel in Vic's hands, a boulder they had to ease around while brush scrabbled ratlike at Dale's door. Quickly she tried the radio, and there was nothing but static on all the stations. She looked at Vic's grim expression, then out where the headlights slashed into the woods and vision was like a solemn series of dimly lighted slides: gray boles and wormlike brush frozen in the act of grasping at throats, a lonely fir among hickory and elm like a fur-cloaked woman in the middle of a slum, an opossum crawling unconcernedly in front of the car like some great gray slug, and the quick white flick of a running deer's tail.

An abrupt gust of wind that sent armies of leaves into the air, spinning dead dervishes at the side of the road.

"This is insane. It's just too insane to be real!"

"We heard what we heard."

"Then we're hysterical or something. We have to be! We've given our minds, our imagination some kind of preconception and now everything's being colored by it. I know what it was, some kind of hallucination!"

"An aural hallucination?"

"It happens, doesn't it? People hear things all the time. They hear voices. They hear little men who aren't there."

"Dale, Jaimie was there. So was Ed. And Ed was,

God help me, afraid of him. His own small son, and he was afraid of him in there.''

A bird darted in front of the windshield, and Dale screamed before she could recognize the intruder. Vic tried a small laugh, but when she answered it, it was more like a choking.

"Spooky up here, isn't it?"

"Vic, are you running away or looking for someplace where we can have space to do some thinking?"

"I wish I knew."

Finally the road completed its contortions, straightened, and began a steep climb. The forest moved closer, and Dale thought it would take only a year or two more of continued neglect before the trees took over and the road became an unscheduled dead end. Not a bad fate, she decided; but before she could say something to Vic the trees thinned and fell back and they were at the summit of a low hill somewhere to the north and east of the village. The road stopped, and Vic was forced to make an awkward U-turn, halting in the middle of the road, facing back the way they had come. The headlights soared off into nothing, the tips of the trees below them barely touched by the spears of white. Despite the heater and its fan, Dale shivered. Vic switched off the lights, and there was only the dashboard glow. She felt, then, as if she were in a miniature submarine fathoms deep, where fish carried their own illumination and monsters as yet unseen were trapped by the pressure in the depths far deeper than black.

"Why did we go there?" Vic asked, shaking his head. "Whoever's idea that was ought to be shot."

"Bang," she said, pointing a forefinger at him. He didn't laugh, however, and she didn't blame him.

"So tell me why I thought we should go there."

"The idea was to confront Ed, remember? Supposedly we would right now be better able to understand what's going on around here. Unfortunately, through no fault of your own, I'm worse off than before."

"You and me both, lady."

They looked straight ahead.

"God, that voice!"

"Please, Dale, don't remind me!"

Over the invisible hood into the darkness unrelieved by stars or distant towns' lights. And for the lack of those lights it was far colder than the frost that already formed brittle lace edges on the windshield.

"Do you think Jaimie's possessed, Vic? Do you think something's got hold of him and makes him the way he is?"

"I can't get myself to believe that was him talking. Is that the same thing?"

He turned on the motor again, letting the heat wash over them ineffectively before bringing back the silence.

"If Ed is so scared of whatever's going on there, maybe we can talk him into helping us. Maybe we can meet him someplace away from Jaimie and talk to him again. He must want to help us, Vic. He's much too intelligent not to want to get out of whatever it is he's involved in."

"To tell you the truth, kid, I don't think Jaimie will let him go."

"You've got to be kidding!"

"I hate to be redundant, Dale, but you heard what

I heard. Did that sound as if he would let his father go?''

''Now listen, possessed or not, he is still a little boy! Ed must be at least six feet tall, if not more. He slumps so much you can't tell. But, Vic, he's bigger and he's the boy's father! How can he stop his own father from walking out if he wants to?''

Vic tapped her wrist. ''How did he stop Dave?''

In the air above the road.

''I wish I knew what was going on. I wish I understood. Maybe we ought to see Fred. Who cares what he thinks! Just tell him, so if something else happens he'll know.''

''And what will he do?''

She made a fist, slammed it on the dashboard. ''How should I know! He can arrest Jaimie—''

''Dale!''

''—or Ed or Flora or . . . how should I know? All I know is, I want to find a nice warm cave somewhere and have a good cry. Is that all right with you?''

In the air above the road.

''Only if I can crawl in with you.''

In the air above the road. Dale blinked, feeling as though she had been without substantial sleep for two weeks in a row. She put a knuckle to her eyes and rubbed. Hard. Wiped a sleeve over her face.

In the air above the road a single yellow glow.

She glanced at Vic. His hands were clenched tightly around the steering wheel, back straight, chin jutting forward. He was staring, mesmerized.

The single yellow glow became a flame hovering steadily some one hundred yards ahead of them. Dale thought at first it was someone walking up the road carrying a small torch; but when Vic suddenly yanked at a knob and the headlights flared on . . . there was only the single yellow flame.

"Swamp gas," she said without thinking.

"Tell me another, Dale, and maybe I'll believe that one, too."

She watched the flame, knowing there was a wind and wondering why it wasn't blown out.

"Is it Jaimie?"

"How can it be?" Vic's voice was low, strained, edged with a fear Dale prayed wouldn't be there. "I mean, how could he have found us? We're in the middle of nowhere, for crying out loud. He couldn't have run behind us all the way. Nobody can run that fast, nobody!"

"Is it Jaimie, Vic? Please. Is it Jaimie?"

"Oh, Jesus, Dale, I think so."

The flame rose to clear the level of the trees. It steadied. It multiplied. Two . . . four . . . a blaze that made no sound. In the amber glow around it, there was smoke. Whirling as if it was trapped by the fire. Puffing into a cloud that moved steadily toward them, bringing the fire on its back like a rider. Sparks like shooting stars, red and amber. The cloud slowly broadened as the fire slowly expanded, and they could feel the heat as it penetrated the car. Vic frantically tried the engine—it coughed once and died.

A nightbird flew out of the woods, wheeling about the cloud. A curling hand of soundless fire reached out and grabbed it, and the bird exploded into ash, and the ash fell in slow-motion rain, each fragment flaring once as it struck the cold ground.

Vic, his eyes still forward, reached into the back and grabbed a jack and handle from the seat. He laid the metal across his lap, touching it, fondling it as a second bird tried to dart under the cloud and was snared in a cage, amber and red. The cage shrank, soundless in its fire, and the bird exploded into a comet's tail that drifted to the ground, and vanished.

The stupor that held Dale shattered, and she screamed once before twisting around and fumbling with the door. It fell open and she tumbled outside, into a heat too much like a furnace. Instantly Vic scrambled over the seat and knelt beside her, shouting into her ear, then grabbing her elbows and jerking her to her feet. She slapped at his face, punched his chest, screaming, crying, until she yielded to his strength and let him lead her around to the back of the car. Watching as the cloud-and-fire drifted to within fifty yards, still expanding though its light was contained and did nothing to dispel the blackness around them.

A wind they couldn't feel boiled into the fire, twisted it, molded it, separated it into a monstrous image of black eyes and black mouth; and in the eyes, a single glowing flame, and in the mouth, a reflection of the cloud outside.

Dale tried to cover her face and banish the flames into the nightmares of her imagination. But it was futile, and her hands dropped limply to her sides. The fire was too fascinating, too compelling to avoid or ignore. And she was quietly resigned to remaining where she was. Behind the car. On the ground. Running now would only prolong the apparently inevitable, and she was too tired to tell herself not to give in.

The cloud/fire/visage halved the distance between itself and the car. Vic, grunting against the heat that pressed him down, flung both handle and jack at the approaching conflagration, but they fell short, vanished into the darkness without a sound to mark their feeble descent.

Dale, swaying, put her hand to the trunk and snatched it away. The car was too hot to touch, and she whimpered, blew on her palm, and didn't protest when Vic put an arm tightly around her waist and backed her with him toward the edge of the road. He said something, and she nodded, though she didn't know what he was talking about, could barely hear anything but the sound of her breathing.

Then the cloud grew, the fire gave itself voice—a muted roar that sounded like an angry giant's humming.

The gas tank exploded. Dale screamed. The flames on the road reached out to the flames in the sky and they joined, billowing, red and amber, at last permitting light to escape them. Dale ducked away, her vision momentarily seared by the glare. And when she could see, she turned Vic around to face her, to look at her one last time. She thought he was crying and wanted to kiss away the tears, but his coat was jammed up between them and she pushed at it frantically, needing now to feel him closer. She pushed and slapped a lump in his pocket. He shouted something, but it was lost in the roaring, the fire, the heat of the cloud that extended thick fingers above them. There was something in the coat that was keeping them apart. Something in the coat. She didn't want it, couldn't have it come between her and Vic and the coming immolation. She glanced up and saw his eyes closing, knew his strength had finally gone and the dizziness had at last returned. He sagged and she held him, felt the lump again and snatched at it furiously, screaming her anger, pulling it out and raising her hand to fling it away. Stopped. And stared at it.

Wood. Carved. The Hound of Culann. McPherson had slipped it into Vic's coat before they had left the house. There was no need for Jaimie to chase after them; he knew that whatever guided and fed that fire would follow the Hound and destroy its holder.

Willy.

Dave.

The heat dried her face, her lips, scorched the tips of her hair. She felt a slight burning sting at her forehead and the backs of her hands.

Suddenly she snapped her gaze away from the face in the cloud and threw the Hound to where the car had once been. Then she held Vic's arm with both hands and tugged him until they broke into a trot, a run, ignoring the lances that thrust at her legs as they moved off the road and into the underbrush. A small branch struck Vic's forehead and he shook his head, looked at her dumbly until her shouts and gestures penetrated. Into the trees, then, and downhill. Careening off trunks, falling head first into brush that snapped off twigs into her cheeks and palms, spinning away from half-buried boulders that numbed her ankles and brought agony to her soles.

And above them, still on the summit, the cloud/fire imploding. Through the branches she watched it drifting. The roaring ceased. The face vanished into flames again. The cloud evaporated into whirling smoke. The smoke that sparkled bright red and amber was sucked into four, into two, into a single yellow flame that became a bright glare, a glow, a point of light that could have been a star.

And it was dark.

Still running, Dale tripped over a black thing and this time her hands and arms would not bring her back to her feet. Vic followed directly behind her, landed on her back and knocked the air from her lungs. She tried a scream; she could only grunt before the lack of air and the wash of pain and the overwhelming relief of escape became too much, too soon, and she allowed herself to black out in a single grateful step.

# CHAPTER
# XII

The clouds broke, and there was a moon. The light
and the air were cold—a soothing chill reminiscent of
a dive into a pool on the hottest summer day. Dale
smiled, wishing the bed wasn't so hard, but when she
twisted to her side the mattress turned to rock. An
initial refusal to open her eyes was immediately coun-
termanded by the sudden fear that something had
happened to Vic. She lifted an arm to brush over her
face, lowered it and saw him sitting at her feet on a
platform of stone. His forearms were resting on his
knees, his hands clasped. Watching. Patiently waiting for her to regain consciousness. When she smiled
he moved swiftly to her side and grasped both her
hands, ran two gentle fingers over her cheeks. She
winced, but grabbed his wrist before he could pull
away.

"How are you feeling, lady?"

"I ache, but what a great feeling."

"I know what you mean."

After a first abortive attempt that sent them sprawling, he managed to bring her to her feet, and they stood uncertainly, not wanting to but unable to avoid gazing toward the top of the hill.

"It really was there, wasn't it?"

He nodded. "I snuck back up when it was obvious you weren't going to come back for a while." A hand rubbed at his beard. "There is nothing there at all, Dale. No ashes, no fumes, nothing. The stupid road isn't even scorched. We might as well have not even been there for all the evidence there is left."

"Now that's just great! I was hoping we could finally go to Fred and tell him what's happening."

"Not now, lady. There's no way."

"Yeah, so what else is new?"

The cloud, face, fire, smoke—she shuddered as reaction finally broke through the control of her limbs, and she leaned against him until the moment had passed, the images were locked in some distant vault. There were tears on her cheeks, but she couldn't recall weeping; Vic's coat was stiff with dirt and clinging leaves, yet it was softly comforting and she didn't want to release him.

"Hey," he whispered, "I think it's about time we stopped playing mountain goat and got out of here."

"If I weren't so scared," she said, "I'd jump you so we'd have something to tell the kids."

"What kids?"

"Oh, didn't I tell you about that?"

He laughed, took her hand and led her downward, angling away from the road they had taken with the car. "Sooner or later we're bound to hit the high-way," he explained when she wondered aloud why they didn't take the easy way, "and besides, if you don't mind, I'd just as soon not be around if that . . . thing shows up again."

"It won't," she said, and reminded him of the Hound.

"Beacon," he muttered. "Poor Dave. Poor old Dave."

A deer trail took them part of the way, allowed them time to think as they groped through the pale light with hands outstretched to keep branches and shrubs from slapping at their faces. Several times sudden dips sent them tumbling, but Dale soon learned to relax so that falls were easier when the ground vanished from beneath her feet.

"What was it?"

"If I knew that, madam, I'd know where to start."

A light below them winked. Vic halted their prog-ress for a moment as he stared, bending forward at the waist as if the added inch would ease his vision. Then he moved to his right away from a thick nest of fir.

"Blessed be, street lights! The highway's down there at last. Straight ahead, kid. Third star to the right and all that jazz."

Never-never land, she thought; I should be so lucky.

They clambered over rocks stripped of their moss, climbed over and crawled under fallen trunks glitter-ing faintly with a light gray frost. Their only com-pany the sharp crack of their thrashing, the rolling away of dislodged stones. Dale clung to the sounds,

using them to drive off the persistent faint roaring
that surged with the memory of the thing in the cloud.
She no longer doubted. She no longer gave credence
to the reasonable belief that they had been gullible
victims of some exotic form of malevolent hypno-
tism; if that were the case, the car would still be
where they had left it, and they would be in it now,
riding comfortably back to the village instead of
gouging themselves with unseen branches, thorns,
daggers of stone. Mesmerism didn't leave physical
scars or wounds that bled, didn't scorch a palm or
cause an automobile to explode.

And she knew the acceptance was entirely an act
of desperate faith, a fumbling embrace by her mind
of something previously and undeniably, literally fantastic. It had to be that way. To continue to deny
what her senses and sense demanded would mean the
abdication of her sanity. The acceptance, then, that
became a weapon, something she could use now to
fight back before she was killed.

And killed she would be without it. That, too, was
beyond speculation.

The most difficult thing would be in talking with
others, as talk they must. As she scrambled into a
ditch and pulled herself out, she could see their faces;
as she brushed herself off, she heard the first automobile grumbling past them less than a hundred feet
away. Liz or Fred or Abe or even Bella—their lips,
eyes, hands twisted in pity-filled sympathy as they
wondered what had happened to the girl they had
known, tried to guess at what terrible thing it was
that had snapped the threads binding her to the real
world.

Liz would most likely call it symptoms of the aftershock from the incident in the orchard.

Fred would label it the extreme emotional reaction to the deaths of the Campbells, and the incident in the field.

Bella would snort and call it strain. A young, healthy woman had no business trying to run a thriving store on her own.

She stopped, grabbed onto a pine bough, and allowed herself to sag into a position of temporary rest. Talk they must? No. No, they could not talk, not to anyone. Not until they either convinced Ed McPherson that he would be much safer in exposing everything before it was too late, or until someone else, a third unknown, survived an encounter with the things, the powers that were hovering over Oxrun Station. Until then, they would have to be silent. And the decision, though inevitable, was anguished enough to make her gasp.

She stood on the shoulder in plain view while Vic tried to flag a car out of the oncoming traffic. They had brushed each other off as best they could, plucked leaves and other debris from their faces and hair, but in the middle of this isolated stretch of road, Dale felt sure there wouldn't be a driver brave enough to stop and pick up two people. After fifteen fruitless minutes she suggested she step back into the shadows, but Vic vetoed the idea almost immediately—he didn't want to be hanging onto a car-door handle when she stepped out into view and the car took off.

Another half an hour. They walked. Stopped. Walked still farther along the ankle-wrenching graveled shoulder.

"Maybe I should show them a little of my fabulous legs," she said. "You know, the Gable-Colbert thing in *It Happened One Night*?"

"Hey, what do you want them to do, lady? Speed up?"

She slapped at his arm and they resumed their walking. Five minutes later a car raced past them in the opposite direction. Suddenly it flared its brakelights and made a screeching U-turn.

"I don't believe it," Dale shouted. "A bloody good Samaritan." Before Vic could stop her she stepped into the road and began waving her arms. When he yelled a warning, she ignored him; the idea of getting warm again was worth the praying that the fast-approaching vehicle wouldn't try to run her down. She shouted, semaphored, and the car slowed, easing off the highway onto the shoulder. Its lights were bright, and she hesitated, feeling uncomfortably like a moth trapped and pinned to black glass. Then, her relief too great, she raced forward calling before nearly tripping herself in an attempt to slow down and stop. It was a police car, and the patrolman sliding out of the passenger door had his weapon drawn. The spotlight on the roof glared abruptly, and she raised a trembling hand to shade her eyes.

The only sound was the grumbling of the engine.

"Dale? Dale Bartlett, is that you? Is Vic with you?"

She leaned forward, staring at the dark figure. "Fred?"

"Come over here, Dale. You, too, Vic."

She checked the run she nearly broke into, glanced back over her shoulder, puzzled when she saw the alarm spreading across Vic's face. Suddenly a truck thundered past, its wind whipping the coat about her legs, kicking dust into her face and making her cough. A hand darted automatically to her hair, pushing at it, finding a shard of a leaf and discarding it hurriedly. She reached the car a step ahead of Vic, and she frowned when Fred backed away as he holstered his gun. His hand, however, remained near the butt.

"For crying out loud, Fred, what are you trying to do, give me a heart attack? I'm not a criminal, you know. It's me, Dale!"

Borg said nothing. He opened the rear door and motioned her inside, Vic following silently. There was a mesh screen across the top of the front seat, and when she checked she found no inside handles on either of the doors. By the time she had unraveled her confusion she realized Fred had been speaking on the police radio, letting the dispatcher know who it was he had picked up on the Mainland Road. Vic stared stonily ahead, not changing his expression when Borg twisted around until his back was to his door and he was facing them.

"It's a cold night, Dale. Where have you been?"

She started to tell him, then felt a painful silencing grip on her wrist. "You wouldn't believe me if I told you, Fred. Now would you mind telling me what's going on around here? Are we really being arrested? Why are we being arrested? I don't understand."

"Has anyone else seen you two in the last couple of hours? Anybody at all? Did anyone pick you up?"

"Nobody picked us up, no. Has anyone seen us? I don't know, but not within . . . what time is it?"

"It's going on eleven."

"My God, so late?"

"Come on, Dale, stop—"

"No," Vic said flatly, "no one has seen us except for some drivers who wouldn't stop for us. The only alibi we have, if that's what you're looking for, is each other. And I gather that isn't going to be good enough this time."

"To be honest," Fred said, "I don't know. Look," and he glanced quickly at his driver, "I don't like this any more than you two do. I wish I didn't have to, but it's got to be done. Abe wants you guys in, and I'm lucky enough to happen to be the one who located you. Some of the others might not have been so . . . friendly."

"Stop it!" Dale snapped, yanking her wrist out of Vic's still tight grip. "Will you two stop talking in riddles and tell me what's going on around here? What's all this garbage about alibis and stuff? Why does Abe want us this time? Somebody burn down the school or something?"

"Let me guess," Vic said as if she hadn't interrupted. "We are obviously suspected of something, aren't we? Something more than setting a few half-dead apple trees on fire. It wouldn't be something like murder, would it?"

"Murder?" She turned to Vic, astounded. "Murder? I . . . this is really . . . for God's sake, Vic!"

"It is, Fred, isn't it?"

The radio crackled; the car swerved sharply to avoid a racoon lying dead in the road.

"It was about nine o'clock, something like that," Borg said, his voice strained. "Jaimie McPherson called the station and told the sergeant on duty that Ed had been killed."

"Oh my God," Dale whispered. "Oh my God."

"He was out for a walk, the boy said he was, and when he got back to the house he looked around for his father because he didn't answer his calls. He found Ed's body in the bathtub. It looks as though it was a rotten accident—and that's strictly off the record, damnit—but he claims you two had been there earlier in the evening and that the three of you had one hell of an argument. He says he left before it was over, slipped out the back way. He doesn't know exactly how long he was gone, but when he came back, there was Ed in the bathroom and . . . well, you can see the inference."

"I don't believe it," Dale said. "I mean, I really don't believe this. It isn't happening, is it, Vic? Vic—"

"Hush up, love," he said, putting an arm around her shoulder and pulling her to him.

"But, Vic—"

"Dale, be quiet. Please, love, there's nothing to worry about. We're going to be just fine. Stop worrying, okay? We're going to be all right."

The patrol car turned onto Chancellor Avenue and sped toward the station. Dale, watching the homes blur past, couldn't stop her eyes from tearing, blinking, couldn't keep from swallowing the bile that was surging acrid in her throat. Nightmare within nightmares. A close friend bringing them in for questioning about the death of a close friend. It didn't make sense, and she was stunned into frightened silence as the car pulled into the drive beside the station, stopped and waited. Fred, trying to give them a small smile of encouragement, guided them through a side door, across the front room where he nodded to the sergeant, and directly up the side corridor and into Abe's office. He didn't draw his weapon again, but he and his partner stayed shadow close. And when the door closed, Dale noticed they were making a point of showing her they were still outside.

Stockton was behind his desk. His face was creased and reddened, as if he'd been roused from a sound sleep only minutes before. He needed a shave, and his white civilian shirt was opened at the collar, the sleeves rolled hastily up to his elbows.

He didn't look up from a sheet of yellow paper lying in front of him.

Dale forced a cough into her palm.

"I want to know if Dale and I are under arrest," Vic said, and she noticed immediately the strain of keeping his voice, and his words, deferential. "If we are, Abe, then I would like to make the proverbial phone call and get in touch with a lawyer. We haven't been read our rights yet, you know."

"Hopefully you won't be hearing those," the chief said, finally meeting Vic's gaze, "but I don't think I'd discount that laywer just yet." He shook his head. "Brother, you've done it good this time, you two have. I just hope you can get yourselves out of it."

"I think we can," Vic said. For the first time since they were picked up he smiled. Dale couldn't see the humor, but the gesture served to help her relax—not completely, but enough so that she was far less petrified than she had been when she'd seen Fred's gun wavering in her direction before being put away.

"All right," Abe said. "Now because you two are

friends, and because Oxrun isn't the big city or a miserable little hick town looking for the limelight, I'm going to tell you what we know so far.'' He lifted the sheet closer to his eyes, squinted and set forefinger and thumb to rubbing his chin. ''Jaimie McPherson called in here at exactly nine-oh-eight to report the death of his father. He was, according to the desk sergeant, hysterical and naturally incoherent. Patrolman Borg and his partner answered the call and found McPherson lying in the bathtub. The shower was still running, warm, and the room was steamed up—Jaimie had apparently closed the door again after he saw what had happened. McPherson was bare to the waist, and without shoes or socks. It could,'' he said, looking up, ''very well have been a miserable accident. I say miserable because of the way his wife died. He could have leaned over to adjust the water, slipped—there was some water on the floor by the tub—and struck his head on the tile wall. He could have drowned, or the blow could have killed him. That I couldn't tell anyone just now. We only picked you two up—''

''We know,'' Dale said, surprised she still had a voice. ''Fred told us.''

''Okay, then,'' Abe said, leaning back in his chair. ''Vic, you said you can get yourselves out of this sticky-looking situation. Go ahead.''

''Vic,'' Dale said before he began, ''don't you think we'll need a lawyer?''

''No, not yet,'' he answered, still smiling. Then, to Abe: ''We're not going to deny that we visited Ed tonight. There would be no sense in that. We did. That's a fact. We got there just about eight—Dale heard the clock chiming inside. We didn't stay for more than a half an hour, forty-five minutes tops. I wanted, see, to buy a chess set from him, one he'd gotten from Dale's store. He wouldn't sell, and we argued about it. But it wasn't a screaming match, as Jaimie seems to imply. When we left we decided to go for a ride, so we headed up Mainland for . . . I don't know . . . ten miles or so before we came to a side road that headed up one of the hills. It shouldn't be too difficult to find; it was a couple of miles past that old gas station out there. Anyway, we stopped at the top of the hill to check the view, and I found out I had a flat tire. And wouldn't you know; I didn't have a spare.''

"Dumb," Dale said. "He'd forget his head if it wasn't screwed on.''

"True enough, true enough. Well, we decided to make for the gas station to get some help. Then I discovered I'd left my gloves back in the car, so we turned around and hadn't gone a dozen steps when we heard the engine start. I ran most of the way—''

"Leaving me to stand in the dark," Dale interrupted.

"—but when I got there, there was nothing left but the jack I'd taken out of the trunk.''

Abe stared at him. "What you're trying to tell me is that someone stole your car?''

"Right," Vic smiled. "Probably some kids out for a joy ride or something. Anyway, we turned around again and walked all the way back down the hill to Mainland. Fred should be able to tell you where he picked us up. Abe, there's no way Dale and I could have been at the McPhersons' when Ed was killed. Not and be where we were on the road when Fred saw us.''

"And we want to report a stolen car," Dale added, trying not to grin.

"I suppose you have proof of being up there," Abe said, almost comical in his effort to remain official and express relief at the same time.

"Just send somebody up there to look for our tracks and the jack. The jack should still be there. I didn't feel like carrying it with me. It isn't all that sentimental."

Stockton slapped at the intercom on the corner of his desk, snapped out his instructions and sat back again. "I don't like this," he said, almost to himself. "I don't like this one bit."

"Ed," Dale said suddenly. "That had to be an accident, Abe. Jaimie was rightly upset, finding his father that way. But all he did was strike out blindly. We were the last ones there and the natural ones for him to pick on. I mean, really, Abe—he's lost both mother and father in something less than a few short years, and they both died in the same way. It would be enough to drive anyone hysterical, especially a young, impressionable boy."

When Stockton didn't answer, she looked to Vic and sat in the wooden chair she had used the last time she'd been in the office. She hoped the patrol wouldn't be gone long, prayed that the jack Vic had thrown at the firething was still on the hill. A trembling forced her to clasp her hands tightly in her lap, move them to grab at the armrests. She felt her control slipping in the weighted silence that pressed on her shoulders, and she cleared her throat just to hear the sound. Abe ignored her, began a ritual shuffling of papers, making notes, murmuring into the intercom without looking up; his mime of temporary disinterest was maddeningly stilted, and she wanted to strike out at him, to demand that he punch through the monstrous holes in the fabric of their story and compel them to reveal the truth. Relief. She blinked quickly, leaned slightly to her left to stare at a small travel alarm clock perched on top of the intercom cabinet. She watched the luminous green hands crawling from minute to minute, knowing that the more she looked the slower they would move, yet she was unable to take her eyes away. Only once did she allow herself a glance at Vic, and saw him leaning against the far wall, his expression unemotional, his eyes roving the office an inch at a time.

Suddenly an image imposed itself on the blank wall she had created in her mind: Ed McPherson, glasses askew, forehead bloodied, face distorted under the water flowing from showerhead to drain. A shadow without apparent source darkened . . . stained one wall, a shadow huge and formless, its edges tongues that wavered like a fringe of flame. It had no dimension, yet it lifted from the wall and blotted out the light, blocked the corpse sprawled in the tub for an eon-long moment before receding, shrinking, vanishing into the dark corner behind the door. And the body . . . shriveled, wrinkled as though it had been immersed for hours, tiny threads of blood pink streaking the sides of the tub and dying into clusters of blackened scab.

There was a stench. Putrefying flesh.

Dale gagged and opened her mouth to scream, would have done so had not the door opened suddenly and a patrolman poked his head into the office.

He looked from Vic to Abe to Dale, and back to the chief again.

"What is it, Simmons?" Stockton growled.

Simmons edged into the room, nodded to Dale and placed a large object wrapped in brown paper on the desk. He leaned over and whispered into the chief's ear, answered a single curt question with a one-word answer and left. The door closed without a sound.

"Well?" Vic said.

Color returned to Stockton's face. He tore open the package and Dale closed her eyes, slumped in her chair and wiped a palm across her forehead.

"I told you it would be there," Vic said, pointing to the jack and its handle.

"They found it off to the side of the road."

"What can I say? I got so mad that I threw it. It sure wasn't going to do me any good without the car."

Abe rose, slowly, and leaned forward, his hands firm on the desk top. "Vic, Dale, there are a lot of people in this little town that I never expect to see in here, or out there," and his head jerked in the direction of the front desk. "I would have bet my life that you two belonged to that select group." Then his hand lifted quickly. "Hold it, Dale! Don't say anything. Not yet. What I'm trying to say is this: we get our share of noncrimes around here—accidents, crank calls, things like that—and it beats me why you of all the people I could think of have gotten yourselves involved with so many of them. It was getting very annoying, and now it's deadly. You're probably right, Dale, and the kid was most probably hysterical over the circumstances of Ed's death. Borg sure made it sound that way when he reported in; and though I haven't spoken with the boy myself, I'll do that first thing in the morning, if he's calmed down some. I have him staying with some people who came right over when the boy asked me to call.''

"Who?'' Dale asked.

Abe waved the question away. "What I want to know is this: are you two involved in something I should know about? I mean, coincidences are fine in their place, and there are folks who have, for example, traffic accidents a couple times a year just because they have plain rotten luck. But when I see you, Dale, in here more times in the last five months than in your whole life, I begin to wonder. And can you blame me?''

He waited, looked at them expectantly. Dale moved to Vic's side and took his arm, held on, and waited for him to say something.

"Can you blame me?'' Abe repeated.

Vic remained calm. "No, Abe, I can't blame you at all. Look, the last time we were here we had words. But that was, I think, more because of the reaction to that unfortunate fire than because we're actually hostile toward you. And I certainly don't want words with you now. This is too serious for that. You're just going to have to take my word for it that there's nothing going on, nothing at all except, as you say, plain rotten luck that's mixed us up in this mess.''

"Your story leaves something to be desired, Vic.''

Dale caught her breath.

"But even if I wanted to—and I don't—there's not much I can do about it now. This,'' and he jabbed a finger at the jack, "and Jaimie's emotional state, and your good characters—if I can use such an outdated term—seem to let you off the hook. Not that you were seriously on one anyway."

"So we can go then," Vic said.

"You can go," Abe nodded, "as long as you're sure you're just attracting bad luck."

"I can only say again, Abe, that Ed was a friend of ours."

"All right."

"And if you don't mind," Vic added, glancing at his watch, "I'll wait until morning to fill out whatever reports there are for my car."

Stockton only dipped his head wearily, and Dale backed to the door, opened it and looked up at Borg, whose anxiety was unprofessionally evident.

"I think he wants to see you," she said.

"This is supposed to be your line," Vic said when they stepped outside and flinched at the whipping cold, "but I sure don't fancy staying alone tonight."

Dale said nothing, only took his arm and hurried him the few long blocks to her house. They sat in the living room, staring out the windows, clinging to each other like children in the face of a storm. And when they spoke, it was in whispers—meaningless sentences, nonsense phrases, groping for the comfort that would blanket them against the coming of the dawn.

# CHAPTER
# XIII

"Who," Vic said, "is getting on whose nerves?"

Dale flung a pillow into the corner of the sofa and strode angrily to the front window. "You are getting on my nerves."

Vic laughed harshly, turned up the television and clapped in time to a commercial's jingle.

A prisoner, Dale thought, a prisoner in my own house.

After they had finally awakened—stretched out on the floor and covered by a blanket Vic had fetched from an upstairs closet—they had decided with little disagreement that it would be something akin to suicide to show themselves in the village. Whatever was stalking them might be inclined to do so more boldly, and more effectively, as time drained rapidly toward the first of November. Given the powers preternatural behind the firething, they knew the house would

229

be less than impregnable; yet it easily presented itself as a comfort which temporarily warmed them, a fortress which gave them a tenuous sense of security.

And for the first few hours of the day it worked.

By midafternoon, however, Dale's calm had shredded into a quiet, slow fear. There were no signs of attack, no contact at all with the outside world except for a single curt call to Bella to close the store if she didn't want to work by herself—but the fear grew nevertheless, and as it did it stifled freedom of movement within the house. They had wandered about in acrimonious silence, in ever decreasing patterns until they were caged in the one room, staring out at the traffic, watching the children racing by in their Halloween costumes. The doorbell rang several times, but neither of them felt constrained to answer it. Next year, Dale promised the figures as they fled from the porch, next year I'll have tons of candy; but this year she trusted none of the tiny ghosts and goblins, pirates, and tramps that dragged their paper sacks and pillow cases from door to door in search of their treats.

A prisoner.

Twilight came early, then, with a settling of thick clouds while the air turned a dull gray, a foglike dimness that blurred the wall of the park trees, forced cars to turn on their lights and become furtive things that scurried by the house in search of warmth. By four it was snowing, and by six great flakes had coated bark and shrub, erased the walks, filled the gutters.

"Why don't they do something?"

They were in the kitchen waiting for the kettle to boil.

"I don't understand why they don't do anything."

"They don't have to now," Vic said. "Someone there is smart enough to realize we can't tell the authorities what we suspect. And as long as we don't directly threaten them, they can pretty much leave us alone."

She nodded, not entirely convinced. Then she lifted the kettle from its burner, poured the steaming water into two cups. A frown when she heard Vic begin a quiet laugh, a turn when the laugh quickly built into a full-throated howling that made his eyes water and forced him to sit at the table before he fell. She glared, hating to be left out of the joke, shouted to calm him down and received only a trembling, pointing finger in return. The cups. She glanced down into the clear water. She had forgotten to spoon in the instant coffee.

"That does it!" she said, and stamped out of the room.

Vic followed, still laughing, and put his arms around her, hugged her tightly.

"We can't just sit here, Vic," she said into his chest. "If I'm not crazy now, I definitely will be before the day is over."

He nodded, gasped for a quieting breath before releasing her and grabbing the phone book from an end table. He winked and dialed and she listened as he ordered a rental car from the agency two doors down from the toy store. When he finished, he grinned.

"In an hour. The guy said he'll bring it over, which is what I call typical Oxrun hospitality."

She hesitated before responding. To begin some sort of action was at the moment infinitely preferable

to remaining in the house—but now that the moment
had come she wasn't sure precisely what it was that
should be done. And immediately as she thought it
she knew it was a lie.

"How are you feeling?"

She shrugged. "Better, I guess. Better than sitting
around, anyway."

"Good." He slapped at his knees. "Now, the first
thing we'll do is get something decent to eat. There's
no sense in launching an attack on an empty stomach."

"Vic, do you have to use that word?"

"What word?"

"Attack."

His hand reached to her shoulder, turned her and
pushed her lightly toward the kitchen. He said nothing, and there was nothing to be said. Only the sounds
of the pots on the stove, dishes on the table, refrigerator humming. She tasted little but ate well, surprised
that her stomach could be so receptive at a time like
this. And while Vic was upstairs hunting for warm
clothing, she stood at the sink with her hands immersed in warm soapy water, watching the storm
outside. The snow had changed over to smaller flakes,
a laced curtain that slapped icily against the window
pane. When the doorbell rang she didn't move, listening as Vic rushed down the stairs and flung open
the door. Voices. Low. Vic's too-hearty laughter and
the door closing again. The water grew cold, the
dishes were unwashed. She saw a darkness between
the flakes that swirled against the direction of the
wind, and in that darkness the presence of the firething.

"Hello, Fred, this is Vic. I thought you'd be out
prowling for ghosts tonight."

"In this kind of weather? You've got to be kidding. Say, how are you two doing? I mean—"

"We're hanging in there, Fred, hanging in there. I'm going to be at Dale's for the rest of the evening. I don't want to get Abe's dander up again. I really don't fancy spending Thanksgiving in one of his hotel rooms."

"Very funny. Hey, you might like to know, by the way, that the prelim medical report confirms Ed's death as an accident. No signs of funny business anywhere."

"That's the best news I've heard all day, pal. All year, in fact."

"I thought you'd like it. But look, my kids are getting ready for a party. I don't want to rush you but . . ."

"Oh, sure, that's all right. Listen, Dale and I were worried about little Jaimie."

"Didn't Abe tell you? He's staying with friends of the family. He'll be all right."

"Oh, that's great. Well, we were thinking, see, of bringing him something from the store. You know, a small gift to keep his mind off things. If you know what I mean."

"Now that's really nice of you guys, Vic. I don't suppose Abe would mind me telling you, then. When the Doc finally got him calmed down, he asked him to call the Campbells. You know the ones—the two old ladies that lost that boy and the father? He's over there now. I don't guess they'd mind you stomping in with something. It is Halloween, after all."

"The Campbells. Oh yes, I think I know where they live. Well, thanks a lot, Fred, and don't let those kids confuse you with the donkey."

"Not me, kid. I just stand around taking pictures like every other father in the world."

Dale shivered in spite of the heater's hard-blowing fan. Boys and girls together, she hummed, me and the Children of Llyr. The houses drifted by slowly as Vic hunched over the wheel, cursing the storm. After the call to Borg, they had thrown on sweaters, coats, boots, and gloves in a tacit decision to make their first move at the Campbell house. Playing it by ear, Vic had called it, and she could think of no other way to do it. Not at least until they knew exactly what was being planned for the Feast of Samain.

Vic grunted.

They were six blocks from Dale's house, the park still on their left. She pointed at a street sign. "Three houses in, I think," she said.

Vic took the corner at a crunching crawl, yet the car still fishtailed when it struck a patch of ice and Dale held her breath until he brought the vehicle back under control. They drove down to the next corner, turned and parked in front of the house just below the Campbells'. The entire street was dark save for the lights in the Campbell windows; it was a low, single-story home; no blanket of snow could adequately hide the fact that it grimly needed a coat of paint.

"Company's coming," Vic whispered, tugging at his gloves.

"Surprise, surprise," she said. "Now what? Do we ring the bell?"

"What do you think?"

With the engine silent the heater wasted no time blowing in cold air. Dale quickly flicked it off, leaned close to her window, and stared. "I think," she finally said, "we'll end up like Ed if we walk in unannounced. We might be able to look in from the side. Let's try it and see who all we can find. Then maybe we'll ring the bell."

"Or run like crazy."

"Or that too," she said, and pushed open her door before she could change her mind.

The front edge of the lawn sloped sharply, the steps leading to the walk uncleared. Dale led the way, angling away from the porch to the side of the house and out of the direct force of the wind. Brushing a glove over her face to wipe away clinging snow, she gripped the sill and raised herself onto her toes while Vic moved down to the next window. She was looking into a small dining room evidently prepared for a Halloween party: streamers dangled from a cheap, brass-plated chandelier; decorated paper plates and cups were placed carefully on a small square table covered with an orange cloth. A plastic pumpkin served as a centerpiece and on the walls were cutouts of witches and cats and small grinning skeletons. But there was no one in the room; nor, as she looked across the front hall, in the room on the other side of the house that she could see. Quickly she rejoined Vic who shrugged failure, and they paused, crouching against the wall as a plow clanked by, before moving cautiously to the back, up onto a narrow porch that faced a treeless back yard. Leaning over the shaky railing, Dale peered through the rear window and saw no one, reached out and gripped the doorknob. A sudden wet gust blinded her, and she waited patiently until the wind calmed. Then she turned her hand.

"Bingo," Vic whispered.

Without bothering to shake the snow from their coats or boots, they stepped into a large white kitchen unremodeled for at least two decades. The stubby refrigerator and bulky stove were a yellowed white, the cabinet doors over sink and counters warped open. There was a battered wooden table in the center of the grease-crusted linoleum floor, and a clock over the entrance to a hall had stopped at seven.

Melting snow dripped down her neck and Dale shook her head, snapped off her scarf and brushed at it. She exhaled. Her breath smoked in front of her. She removed one glove and lay her hand on the radiator by the door—but there was no heat there, no heat anywhere.

Gestures, then, since neither was willing to break the silence that smothered the house. Dale nodded rapidly. A rapid search of the house might bring them luck, and the clues they would need to locate the Campbells. Slowly, then, as though the uncarpeted floor would give way beneath them, they passed through the dingy kitchen into the hall and down to the front. The dining room was as she had seen it from the outside—empty, ready for a party, but without its celebrants.

A staircase formed the right-hand wall of the corridor. She leaned on the newel post, looked upward but saw and heard nothing.

She moved right to stand at the threshold of the living room.

It was far larger than she had first thought, stretching along the full side of the house. There was little furniture, and what there was had been shoved up against the whitewashed walls, off the worn red carpet that only accentuated the grime on the floor. At the far end of the room, however, was a single gold table over which was suspended a small wooden wheel rimmed with lighted candles; they were the only source of illumination in the room, and their spawn of shadows flickered on the walls though the flames were steady.

"Dale," Vic said suddenly, and he pointed.

On the table was the chess set she had sold to McPherson. All the pieces were in place except for a handful of pawns—four were arranged behind the Children of Don, and a fifth was missing.

Dale followed Vic to the table, more like a regal display far out of place in the house it was set.

"Four Hounds," she said dully. "Ed, Willy, Elinor, Dave."

"The one that's gone. It must have been the one I threw at the fire."

She reached out to pick up a queen, snatched her hand back when it met a cold so intense her fingers were burned. She glanced up at the ringed fire, frowning, then opened her eyes wide and took a step away.

"What?" Vic said.

"That ring," she answered. "Like the orchard, Vic. It just now occurred to me," and she struck her forehead with a scolding palm. "Someone tried to kill us out there, right? But unless that fire would have trapped anyone who went there—"

"Someone had to know we would be the ones! But that's silly, Dale. Nobody knew."

"Wrong," she said. "Come on, let's go someplace where it's warm. My ears are ready to fall off.''

She hurried away, was stopped in the foyer when Vic grabbed her shoulder. "Hey, wait a minute! What do you mean, wrong? Who knew, for Pete's sake?''

"Who gave us the list for the scavenger hunt?''

Vic's gesture of denial was stopped by a rustling in the dining room. Dale looked to Vic, hoping to see a signal that would send them running for the safety of their car. But a figure in a billowing black robe girdled in gold stepped into the light and stopped her. The white-trimmed hood was back, the hair straight and wafting in the drafts that eased down the hall. A pale white hand lifted, and there was a gun pointed at Dale's chest.

"Who indeed,'' the figure said. "It's cold out here, children. Please,'' and the gun motioned them into the dining room, into two chairs placed at the head of the table. Liz Provence sat opposite them, her grin a mockery of the pumpkin's plastic expression.

"I don't believe it,'' Vic said finally.

"Why?'' Liz said. "Did you really think you belonged at my party? A schoolteacher and a shopkeeper? Really, Victor, I thought you were smarter than that.''

"I almost started to like you,'' Dale said softly. "I really did.''

"I'm flattered,'' the woman said. She rested her forearms on the tablecloth, keeping the weapon aimed over the top of the centerpiece. "But it's of no consequence now, is it? I mean, the party's over,'' and she waved her free hand at the decorations, laughed loudly in a voice that belonged to a woman ten times her age.

"Samain," Vic said.

Liz quieted abruptly, her face more graven than the chessmen she guarded. "Samain," she said, nodding. "Midnight."

Time, then, and Dale was glad she hadn't worn a watch. The silence became a weight, fought the pressure of the wind, the sound of an occasional passing car. Chills swirled around her ankles, drifted up the legs of her jeans and tightened her skin. She dared not look at Vic for fear she'd cry out, but she knew he was almost numbed by the danger pointing directly at his chest. She coughed once and the gun jerked, and she closed her eyes to wait for the explosion.

"A couple of hours, less," Liz said finally.

"To what?" Dale asked, her voice cracking, her hands tight in her lap. "What's going on?"

"Ah, I thought you knew already. I thought little Willy told you."

"He never had the chance," she snapped. "The children did it, didn't they? He was given one of the pawns, and they drowned him. Samain was what he wanted to tell me about, wasn't it?"

"In one of his self moments, yes, I imagine it was."

The house trembled at a prolonged rush of wind.

"Do we get an explanation?" Dale asked again. "Don't you think we deserve one?"

"A dying request?" Liz said. "No. Not a single word."

"It isn't necessary," Vic said. He pushed back his

chair and stood, carefully, his hands wide to show Liz he had picked up nothing threatening. Slowly he moved to the window, turned and leaned back against the sill. "Samain. When the gods walk, isn't that right? I didn't believe it at first, you know. I thought Dale here was losing her mind. But . . ." and he shrugged into Liz's silent laugh. "Flora brought the means over here, didn't she? Some kind of rituals she unearthed, probably literally, back in Wales or wherever the hell she came from. Something . . . preliminary to possess the children, to give the Children of Don and Llyr some minimum contact with the modern world."

"Those questions," Dale said, striking the table with a palm. "All those questions and sessions with the library. But why the children?"

"Because," Vic said before Liz could speak, "they still have illusions, dreams, fancies and such. Not like us big, sophisticated adults so terribly fashionably cynical that we don't even believe in Santa Claus any more. They would accept the children, wouldn't they, Liz? And that acceptance gave them the foothold they needed."

"But why you?" Dale asked Liz. "I see about the children, but why you and Dave and the others?"

Liz, suffering the conversation with only expressions of congratulations flashed in her face, frowned. She shifted the gun to her other hand and brushed at her hair, smoothed at her cheeks. Her lips were drawn tight, a sneer rather than a smile. Another façade, Dale thought suddenly. Liz wasn't nearly as calm or as brave as she was pretending—somewhere within there was a doubt, a nagging uncertainty about the course she had taken. Most likely she had been promised something for her part in this: immortality, wealth, power, whatever form her greed had taken. Now she was afraid that the payments for her loyalty wouldn't be met. Had Dave and Elinor been that afraid, too, and had they threatened to expose the cult and scatter the influence Flora had so painstakingly gathered? Had it been the chilling effects on the children that had changed their minds, and caused their deaths? It had to be! It had to be that, or why would Dave take the chance of bringing the chessmen to the store, insist that a traveler buy them instead of a Station local? What a relief it must have been to Flora, she thought bitterly, when McPherson rescued them.

"You're doing a lot of thinking, Dale," Liz said sweetly. "Have you decided I'm insane?"

"Insane or not, I feel sorry for you," Dale answered. "If it really happens, if those so-called gods really do come back from their . . . I don't know . . . hibernation, what makes you think they'll pay any attention to you? You've done what you were told, except for killing us. They won't need you any more."

"Nonsense," Liz flared. She lifted the gun and pointed it like a finger. "You saw in there . . . in there . . ." She swallowed and closed her eyes to regain control.

And it was all the hesitation Vic needed. He leapt across the table, landed on his chest as one hand vised Liz's wrist and forced the gun up and away while he slid into her and toppled them both onto the floor. Dale backed to the door, watching the two struggle, her own screams added to Liz's when the gun fired harmlessly into the ceiling, again into the wall. And when she saw Vic was in trouble, she ran to the fight and began kicking at Liz's side viciously. The woman shouted obscenities at her, spat in Vic's face, but he slammed her arm to the floor and the gun sprang from her grip. Without thinking, Dale snatched it up, shouting until Vic scrambled free and leaned against the table, panting, gingerly touching the streaks of blood that lined his face.

Liz backed on hands and knees to the wall, using it as a brace to regain her feet.

"Keep her there," Vic said. "I'll look around here for a phone and get hold of Abe or Fred."

"No!" Liz screamed. She launched herself off the wall, sprawled on the table and grabbed at the silverware neatly fanned over festive napkins. When she stood again she was brandishing a knife. "No!" she screamed again and ran at Vic.

"Liz!" Dale shouted. "Liz, stop!"

The woman hesitated, then pulled back her arm to throw the knife. Dale shook her head violently, tears already on her cheeks as she fired the gun. The knife dropped, and Liz was slammed back against the table, rebounded into the wall next to the window. Standing. Mouth opened. Eyes disbelieving. Slumping, then, slowly to the floor, a broad streak of blood gleaming on the woodwork.

"My God," Dale whispered, and the gun fell from her hand. "My God."

"She was insane," Vic said, taking her arms and holding her against his chest. "Insane. You . . . saved my life, kid. You couldn't have done anything else."

"They're using the children," she said. "Vic, they're using the children."

"We'll find them," he insisted. "Don't worry, Dale, we'll find them and bring them home. They must have told the parents they were going to have a party. Like Fred, they were going to have a party."

Dale stared at the blood on the wall, felt nausea fighting to rise in her throat. But there was no time. She had too much to do before she could react to what she had already done.

"Dale? You okay?"

"Come on," she said angrily, and ran into the living room, swept the chessmen into her pockets, giving those that didn't fit to Vic. "Remember," she said as she hurried him outside, "what you read to me in the library, how those things supposedly come into the world?"

It was a moment before he nodded, halted at the top of the steps and looked up and down the street. She knew what he was thinking. Knew, and hoped whatever other parties there were wouldn't be interrupted.

They headed west on Chancellor, the road still slippery but cleaner now that the plows were working regularly.

"We'd better get there in time," she said once, nodding at the dashboard clock. "It says only an hour, but you never know with these things. I never had a car clock that worked for more than a day."

Vic only grunted.

Had events not been so separated by time, had not so much . . . but she reminded herself that she'd plowed that ground before. The reality was whispers in the park, bonfires, deaths, the firething on the hill—and in the burnt-out orchard a *sid*, a doorway for the Children of Don. No matter that centuries had buried them under a cloak of mythology; no matter that science would, right to the end, deny their possibility, deny their power. She didn't care then what derision might be born in the rest of the world—she knew what she had been through, and she knew the consequence of her failure.

And if she was successful, no one would know about it, and it would be just as well. There were enough nightmares to go around; the world didn't need another.

Ignoring the probability that a patrol car would spot them, they parked on the far shoulder of the highway and scrambled across the drainage ditch and through the hedging into the field. Here there was little protection, and the snow lashed into their faces, stinging ears and nose, burning eyes, and drawing breath cold from their lungs. They held hands to keep from being separated, fell too many times for Dale to keep count; her limbs grew numb, her arm a wooden shield that gave her the illusion of seeing through the storm.

A light, then, wavering in the distance.

The wind, screaming.

The light steadied. A fire in the air. Dale stiffened, shrank back, but Vic yanked at her arm and she allowed herself to be guided to the outer trees, those not destroyed by the first fearful blaze. He cupped his hands around her ear. "They're all there, I think," he said, and she nodded. Despite the storm she could see the children standing around the mound, the *sid*, in what had once been a place of cheering young dreams. They were dressed in black robes with cowls drawn up, motionless and silent.

Three more paces and Dale blinked. A barrier of some sort kept the storm out of the orchard. Suddenly it was warm again. No snow fell, the ground was bare.

And in the air over the *sid*, stark against the black and white night, a single yellow flame.

How much time, she wondered, feeling Vic pressing close as he stared at the tableau. He was waiting for her instructions; after all these months, the moments that had kept them together and apart, he was waiting for her to make the first move, to tell him that what his eyes were seeing, what his mind was denying, was too much the truth. She shook her head, rubbed self-consciously at her side and felt the bulge of the chessmen in her pocket. Somehow these talismans had to be used to a purpose directly opposed to their original intent. She gnawed at her lower lip, tasted the salt blood that broke through the chapped skin. She licked. Glanced back over her shoulder and saw the storm thundering its silence over Oxrun Station.

A movement caught her eye.

Flora glided into the circle. She was dressed in a dull white robe, dull in contrast to the vivid whiteness of the hair that flowed to her waist. Age had been driven from her hands and face, and she was beautiful. A woman carved from a timeless block of unsullied ice.

Priestess, Dale thought, too numbed by the sight to move, to breathe, to cry out her anger.

Flora held out a hand and Milly broke through the circle, held it while the woman climbed assuredly to the top of the mound, smiled down at the children, and lifted her palms toward the single yellow flame.

The children removed their cowls.

Vic fumbled for the lapels of his coat, hung on tightly as though without them he would fall.

Jaimie. Carl. Melody. Debbie. Carol.

They each chose a large stone from the slope of the mound. Milly's face was raised toward the sky, her expression hidden, her hands stiff at her sides. Carl threw first, followed swiftly and accurately by the others. Milly crumpled to the ground, arms jerking to a silent turn, her head crushed, her blood staining the earth, the robe, the tired gray of her hair.

The single yellow flame multiplied—two, four, an inferno.

The cloud. The face.

The giant's roaring.

Flora clenched her fists, spread her fingers wide, wove a sonic pattern in a voice that was the sound of midnight that captured all Time, summoning her Children to take the children waiting patiently at her feet.

The pain in Dale's lip finally broke through the stupor that had entrapped her, and she reached into her pocket. The ground beneath her feet suddenly became warmer, tinted a faint red that spread from the base of the *sid* like a flameless fire. A trembling, then, and a rumbling that could have begun as far away as the stars. Small rocks slid off the mound and gathered at the children's feet. Flora remained unmoving, the cloud/face/fire like a globe suspended above her hands.

A fissure opened along the top of the mound.

Dale yanked out the carving her hand had taken and, with a look to Vic that disrupted his trance, she screamed out Willy's name and flung Govannan, Llew, the fortress Gower into the face of the growing apparition, urging Vic to do the same, watching as the chessmen fed the fire, became fire themselves in raging conflagration.

The rumbling increased and Dale lost her footing, fell back against a tree, and slid to the ground with her arms wrapped tightly around the bole. Vic pitched backward into the storm and lay still, his head propped at an ugly angle, his face quickly whitened by the passing of the snow. Desperately she reached a hand toward him, drew it back when she heard a rising scream.

Flora was struggling with the flame overhead. It was descending, slowly, dropping a cage of fire around her, beneath her. The children backed off, stumbling like drunkards, rubbing at their faces until one of the girls, one of the boys began crying loudly before shifting to screams that matched the agony played out on the *sid*.

The mound ruptured. Thunder, then, and red/amber lightning, and the blizzard ripped through the orchard to cover the earth, hissing, steaming, while Flora sank into the doorway she'd opened; her hair was afire, her robe in charred tatters, her face like a masque of yellow melting wax. Gone to her shoulders, her hands grabbed at the lip of the *sid*, scrabbling, clawing, while the sound of midnight became the pleading of the dying.

The cold returned.

The mound collapsed into a rubble of stone.

And the firething dwindled to a single yellow flame that hovered defiantly before the storm snuffed it out.

Dale watched, wept, then called to the children who ran to her arms and joined in her weeping, shivering in the thin cloth of the robes they wore. Together, then, they carried the still dazed Vic back to the car and brought him to the hospital on the far side of the park. Weeping. And laughing.

And she sat in the waiting room, Jaimie peacefully asleep with his head in her lap. Once the doctors had notified the police, there had been turmoil for several hours while the parents came and went with explanations of drugs and a deranged old woman. Abe had come and gone, but there were no questions, only silent anger and a look of sad bewilderment. Dale promised to see him as soon as she found out how Vic would be, to tell him everything including the body she'd left in the house. If she was believed, and the children stood by her, she would reopen the store and search for a way to soothe poor Bella's feelings.

As if nothing had happened.

As if the fire had never been.

A soft voice paged a doctor.

A patient was wheeled past by two laughing interns.

Vic's doctor stopped to see her, whispered so he wouldn't wake the boy. And she grinned, wiped at her face, brushed a trembling hand through her soaking wet hair.

In a few minutes she would be able to see Vic, to see him and tell him the nightmare was over.

In a few minutes more she would tell him again that she loved him, needed him, couldn't let him go.

And when Jaimie awoke, whimpering until he saw her smile, she cradled him against her breast and rocked him slowly, crooning softly, promising him a new home filled with plants, noisy with television, smelling of food and all kinds of candy.

He laughed and snuggled closer.

She laughed and kissed his forehead.

"Miss Bartlett," he said, "can I have a shelf for my toys and things?"

"You mean those terrible monsters you used to build?"

He nodded; she nodded; and they laughed again, loudly, oblivious to the smiling stares interns and nurses sent their way.

"And Miss Bartlett, can I put this there too?"

And the interns and the nurses stopped when she screamed, raced to restrain her when she threw the boy far from her and began tearing at her hair.

They carried her away, while Jaimie crouched on the floor, smiling, turning over and over and over in his hand a small wooden carving of the Hound of Culann.

## THE BEST IN HORROR